Love's Silent Promise

LOVE'S SILENT PROMISE

♥

NICOLA JAMES

AVALON BOOKS
THOMAS BOUREGY AND COMPANY, INC.
401 LAFAYETTE STREET
NEW YORK, NEW YORK 10003

PRINTED IN THE UNITED STATES OF AMERICA
ON ACID-FREE PAPER
BY HADDON CRAFTSMEN, SCRANTON, PENNSYLVANIA

To Kathleen, who inspired this book,
and to the Ladies of the Group, who made it happen.

Chapter One

It was a hot August afternoon, and Bonnie Delaney was grateful that the air-conditioning in her old blue Nova was working properly for a change. She was surprised by the heavy traffic she encountered in the city of Nashua, New Hampshire, on her way to the small town of Abbots Hill. Once past the city limits, Bonnie was relieved to have the traffic lessen so that she could relax a bit and enjoy the mountain scenery as she wound her way along tree-lined roads. She was trying to remain calm, but she couldn't repress a little flurry of excitement when she thought of the interview ahead. For the first time in her twenty-three years, Bonnie was truly on her own and embarked on an adventure.

* * *

"Bonnie, your dad and I just don't understand why you want to go so far away. You have a perfectly good job right here in Eastboro."

"I know, Mom, but you know I'm not really happy with my job and, anyway, don't you think it's about time I went out on my own?"

"No, I don't. In my day, girls lived at home until they were married."

Bonnie smiled. "Well, that isn't going to happen soon, and besides, this job sounds like just what I'm looking for." She had spread the page of the *Boston Globe* across the kitchen table and had indicated the ad she had circled.

"I don't understand how this day-care center works." Claire Delaney pushed herself from the kitchen table and put the kettle on the stove.

"Well, from what I can understand from Mrs. Hollander, the owner and director, they have forty pre-school children at the center, five of whom are handicapped in some way. My job would be to integrate those five with the other children."

Claire turned from the stove and poured water into a blue teapot. Her expression softened. "How old are these children?"

"Most of them will be under five, I would think."

"Well, that does sound more like what you've always wanted to do," she admitted. "I know you were disappointed when the only job available here was with teenage boys."

Bonnie sighed. "I enjoyed working with the guys, but I really want to work with the little ones." She brightened visibly and stood up to hug her mother. "Please be happy for me, Mom. I'm so excited about this interview. Anyway, I might not even get the job."

Claire sipped her tea. "Of course you'll get the job. Who wouldn't hire my girl?" she declared stoutly.

Now Bonnie turned on to Route 101 and consulted the directions clipped to her visor. *Watch for the sign, Entering Abbots Hill. On your left you'll see Mac-Cready's Farm Stand, and about one half mile farther along look for Red Schoolhouse Day Care.*

Bonnie followed the directions easily and soon found herself pulling into the graveled parking lot of the center. She was surprised to find that the building really was an old schoolhouse. It was at least one hundred years old, and time had tempered the old brick to a mellow shade of pink. It was nearly six o'clock, and the last of the parents were picking up their children. Bonnie sat quietly in her car and watched a burly worker in overalls swing a tiny girl with pigtails up into his arms and carry her to a pickup truck, where he carefully strapped her into a car seat.

When the last of the children were safely on their way, Bonnie emerged from her car and slowly mounted the worn wooden steps. Kate Hollander, the director of the center, had arranged to meet her at six P.M. The nervous flutter returned to the pit of her stomach. She had spoken to Mrs. Hollander several times on the phone and had been impressed by her professionalism, but, since she had imagined her to be a formidable woman, she anticipated a tough interview. Bonnie took a deep breath and walked through the open oaken door.

She found herself in a brightly painted foyer lined with shelves and cubbyholes filled with the belongings of the tiny clients of the center. She peeked into the main classroom, but there was no one in sight. Nervously she called out, "Hello, anyone here?"

"Hi," a cheerful voice called. "Come on through."

Bonnie walked across the wide pine boards streaked with the afternoon sun. She paused in the doorway of a smaller room where a slim girl, dressed in red shorts and a brightly colored T-shirt, was hanging hand puppets on pegs.

"Hi. I'm looking for Mrs. Hollander. I'm Bonnie Delaney."

The girl poked a Big Bird puppet into place and turned with a smile. She walked toward Bonnie with a slim hand outstretched. "Welcome to the center. I'm Kate Hollander."

As Kate Hollander approached, Bonnie could see that she was not the teenager that she had imagined her to be. The slender figure and cloud of brown curly hair belied the fact that Kate was in her mid-thirties. She smiled at the expression on Bonnie's face and looked down at her clothes with a rueful look. "Not quite what you were expecting, am I?"

"Not exactly, I thought you would be. . . ." Bonnie waved her hand helplessly in the air.

"I know." Kate laughed. "I was going to go home and put on my power suit, but then I remembered that I don't have one. I'm afraid you were taken in by my telephone persona, but if I don't assume a professional air, people don't take me seriously. I really am serious about the center and its staff."

Bonnie shook the slim hand and was impressed by its wiry strength.

"Please come into my office. It's really only a converted closet, but sometimes I need to have a place to get away and close a door behind me. You'll find that even our bathroom doors don't lock!"

Kate led the way across the larger classroom to a small room decorated with children's drawings and struggling cactus plants. She sat behind the battered desk and indicated an orange plastic chair for Bonnie.

"Let's talk for a while, and then I'll show you around the building. Tell me why you think you want this job."

Bonnie sat straighter in the plastic chair and pulled her denim skirt down over her long, slender legs. Her brown eyes softened as she thought of how to explain to Kate her desire to work with young handicapped children.

"You have my résumé, so you know that I did my undergraduate work at Fitchburg State College and have my degree in Special Needs. You also know that

I have spent every summer, since I was fourteen, working at a camp for handicapped children.''

"Yes, yes, I have your credentials, and they're very impressive.'' Kate impatiently turned over papers on her desk. "That doesn't tell me why you want this job.'' The voice was familiar. It was the voice from their telephone conversations.

Bonnie squared her shoulders and ran a nervous hand through her soft brown hair. "I want the job for the same reason you run this center. Working with young children with special needs is the only thing I've ever wanted to do!''

"Now that's what I wanted to hear!'' Kate grinned and popped out of her chair. "Now let me show you the center.''

A half hour later Kate looked at her watch and exclaimed, "Look at the time! I have to get home. Mark and the kids will be looking for me.''

"Do you live close by?'' Bonnie asked.

"About ten minutes away. I don't usually stay this late, but when I do, my husband arranges to be home at four-thirty to start supper.''

"How many children do you have?''

"We have three—Sarah, Steven, and Ben. Ben has C.P. He's fairly involved.''

Cerebral palsy, Bonnie thought. "How do you manage?''

Kate smiled gently. "The grace of God and a lot of

energy," she replied. "Ben is the reason I opened the center," she went on. "I was able to keep him with me and still do a job I loved. But he's six now, and it was time for him to move on to another classroom. He's very bright, but physically. . . . Well, you know how it is."

Kate grabbed her bag and keys from her desk and led Bonnie to the front door. On the front steps she paused. "I had planned to bring you down to Mac-Cready's Farm Stand and introduce you to Liz and Tim, but they're expecting you, so you'll be fine on your own. I think you'll enjoy staying with them tonight, and I'll expect you here in the morning about eight o'clock. After you spend a full day at the center, we'll both know for sure whether you're the right person for the job."

With that, she was off the porch and gone. Bonnie watched with fascination as Kate hopped into her red Subaru and disappeared from sight.

Bonnie walked slowly to her car. She had a lot to think about, and she almost wished the drive to MacCready's Stand were a bit longer so that she could organize her thoughts. Being with Kate Hollander was like dealing with a whirlwind. Well, this would be another new experience for her, since she had never stayed at a bed-and-breakfast before or visited a working farm.

Bonnie drove down Route 101 to the farm stand,

where she parked her car and walked between bins of corn, carrots, and cabbage to the screen door. It was not yet seven o'clock, and the humidity still made her cotton blouse stick to her back. It was a pleasure to step inside to the cool, dim interior, where the smells of dried flowers and potpourri mingled with the subtle scent of fresh fruit and vegetables. Behind the wooden counter, Bonnie found a tall, plump woman in her mid-thirties who greeted her with a friendly smile and an inquiring look.

"Are you Liz MacCready?" Bonnie asked.

"Yes, I am. You must be Bonnie. I thought Kate was going to bring you down."

"She was, but she had to get home to her family. She said you would understand."

"Sure, no problem. I was about to leave, anyway." She reached behind the counter and picked up a baby seat and plopped it on the counter. "This little boy is about ready for his dinner."

Surprised, Bonnie gazed at the chubby baby asleep in the little chair, his tiny fists pressed to his dimpled cheeks. His mint-green suit accentuated his pale skin and the wisps of red hair that covered his head.

"He's adorable. How old is he?"

"Just three months. His name is Joshua, but so far we just call him Binky. He was a preemie, and we're lucky to have him at all." Bonnie stroked the baby's face gently with one finger, and he stirred and made a sucking sound.

"Whoops!" Liz said. "I thought he would be hungry. We'd better get him home. Just watch him for a second, will you? I just want to tell Tim I'm leaving."

Liz came from around the counter and walked to the back of the store, where she called out, "Tim, I'm going home to feed Binky. You want to come and mind the store?"

When Liz returned to the front of the store, she was accompanied by a lanky redheaded man. "Tim, this is Bonnie Delaney. No time to chat, but she'll be with us for dinner, which will be in a half hour, so don't let Joe delay you."

Bonnie tried to protest, saying that she couldn't impose on them for dinner, but Liz just shushed her. She scooped up the baby carrier and handed Bonnie a carryall with diapers and sundry other articles in it and hurried out the door with Bonnie in her wake, while Tim just smiled without having said a word.

Bonnie trailed behind her, thinking, *Everyone moves so quickly around here!*

Once outside, Liz said, "Why don't you just leave your car here and ride with me? It will be perfectly safe."

"Fine. Just let me get my overnight bag."

Bonnie grabbed her bag from the backseat of the Nova and locked the car doors. Liz was already heading around to the back of the store, where she opened the doors of a station wagon and quickly placed the baby in his car seat.

"You'll have to ride in back since the Crown Prince has dibs on the front seat. Hope you don't mind."

Bonnie slipped into the backseat, where she smiled at the baby, who had fallen back to sleep sucking on his tiny fist.

Liz started the car and headed up a dirt road that ran behind the farm stand. "The house is only a half mile away," she commented, pointing out signs directing tourists to MacCready's Bed-and-Breakfast.

"Do you get many guests?" Bonnie asked.

"Not so many this time of year, but in late September, when the leaves start to turn, we'll be deluged with 'leaf peepers.' After that there are the hunters, and then in winter a certain amount of skiers."

They pulled up in front of a turn-of-the-century farmhouse with white clapboards that seemed to glow in the twilight. Bonnie helped Liz unload the baby and his paraphernalia and was soon ushered into a spacious foyer graced by simple oak furniture.

"Just drop that stuff and come into the kitchen," Liz said casually. She handed the baby to Bonnie, saying, "See if you can pacify him for a minute while I stir this stew." Liz took the top off a Crockpot, and the savory smell of spices and herbs reminded Bonnie that she was indeed very hungry. She had barely eaten lunch, being so nervous about the interview.

When Liz was satisfied with dinner, she took the baby from Bonnie and settled into an old rocking chair by the window and proceeded to nurse young Joshua, giving Bonnie a chance to examine and admire the spacious room.

"What a charming kitchen!" she commented.

Liz relaxed visibly in the chair and briefly closed her eyes. "Thank you," she murmured.

Feeling like an intruder, Bonnie stood awkwardly for a moment, when suddenly Liz's eyes flew open.

"Sorry," she said. "Nursing is so soothing and about the only peaceful moment I get all day. Please sit down and tell me about your interview with Kate. She's something, isn't she?"

Bonnie perched on a kitchen chair. "Well, if you're sure," she said hesitantly.

Liz carefully placed the baby on her shoulder and coaxed a burp from him. "I'm really interested. Tell all," she commanded, "but first open that cabinet and grab three of those blue dishes and put them on the table."

Between directing the setting of the table and nursing the baby, Liz managed to ask enough leading questions so that Bonnie related the entire interview to her. Suddenly, in mid-sentence, Bonnie paused. "You know an awful lot about the center," she said suspiciously.

Liz laughed as she placed the sleeping baby in a basket. "I was wondering when you'd notice. Kate and I are old friends. We were in college together, and I often fill in at the center when she needs some time off."

"But you're not a teacher, are you?"

"You are confused, aren't you? You thought I was the farmer's wife. Well, I am, but before that I was a sociology major. I met Tim in college. Kate, Tim, and I were all there together. Tim has his degree in music, but when his dad died, we came back here to run the farm, at least until his brother Joe is ready to take over. Joe's in college now, and we want him to finish." Liz put a jug of apple cider on the table and paused as she heard a noise from the back door.

"There's Tim now," she said, "right on time."

Bonnie smiled shyly at the tall man in the doorway. "Nice to have you here, Bonnie. I hear you'll be working at the center," he said, picking up the baby from his basket and burying his nose in the baby's neck.

"I hope so. I don't have the job yet."

"You'll get it, don't worry," Liz assured her. "Tim, don't wake that baby. We'd like to have one civilized meal, if you don't mind."

"I won't wake him," he said contritely. "I just love the way he smells."

Liz smiled fondly at him. "Remember that the next time I ask you to change him," she remarked, placing a tureen of stew on the table.

"Not the same thing at all," Tim replied, carefully lowering the baby into his basket.

"You'll have to forgive us, Bonnie. We're fairly dotty over this baby, but we waited such a long time to have him, and then to almost lose him at birth. . . ."

She wiped a tear from her eye and indicated the place for Bonnie to sit.

They had finished the delicious stew, complemented by whole-wheat bread and sliced tomatoes, and were well into vanilla ice cream with strawberries when the baby woke up, wailing.

"Poor little Binky," Tim crooned, walking up and down the warm kitchen with the baby on his shoulder.

"Why don't you take him inside where it's cooler while Bonnie and I clean up in here?" Liz suggested.

Tim left the room with the crying baby, while Bonnie cleared the table. "Poor little guy," Liz explained, "he has some digestive problems. Fortunately you won't be able to hear him from your room, since we have our sleeping quarters down here. I was worried about that, but none of the guests were disturbed, not even the first few weeks."

"I don't know how you manage all this," Bonnie said.

"It's not that bad, and besides, the bed-and-breakfast is my egg money."

"Excuse me?"

Liz laughed. "You *are* a city girl! The farmer's wife traditionally took care of the chickens and was allowed to keep the egg money for herself. Well, my guests are my responsibility, and I keep the money for myself. You see, I missed working at first. I'm not needed that often at the stand. Tim's mom fills in, and Joe puts in about twenty hours a week. Of course, since the baby came, things have been a little harder, but I'm managing okay.''

Liz gave a final wipe to the counter. ''We're all set here. I'll show you to your room since it sounds like Tim's doing okay with the baby, at least for the moment.''

She led the way down the hall to a wide staircase, leading to the second floor. She paused at the top of the stairs to switch on the hall light. ''We leave this on all night, so feel free to come down if you need a snack or anything.''

Bonnie laughed. ''After that dinner I may not eat again.''

Liz opened the door of the room at the head of the stairs. ''This is our best room. I'd like you to have it for tonight, since we have no other guests until tomorrow night. Then it's reserved for the weekend.''

She lit a bedside lamp, and Bonnie admired the square room with its four-poster bed and warm oak furniture. The two wide windows had lace curtains and the bed, a flower-sprigged spread. There was a wood-burning fireplace on an outside wall.

''It's lovely,'' Bonnie said, placing her bag on the hooked rug at the foot of the bed.

''Thanks. Actually, it's the only guest room with a private bath. The other two rooms have to share the original bathroom, but this bathroom was added many years later. The other one has charm, but this one is convenient.'' She opened a door on the far side of the room to display a compact bath, decorated in shades of blue.

"It's perfect," Bonnie said with delight.

"Good. I'm glad you like it. Then you'll be comfortable here tonight. Why don't you settle in and then come downstairs for a while?"

Bonnie looked at her watch. To her surprise it was almost nine o'clock. "Thanks, Liz, but if you don't mind, I think I'll just stay up here and read for a while. I'm really tired, and I have a lot to think about."

"I understand, and I don't blame you. But, Bonnie, I want you to know, I think Kate would be crazy not to hire you, and I'll tell her so. So if you do decide to take the job, you're welcome to stay here with us and rent this room full-time."

Bonnie was touched. "That would be wonderful, but are you sure that would be all right?"

"Of course. I told you, it's my little project, and I would love to have you here for as long as you would like to stay."

Impulsively Bonnie hugged her. "Thanks, but first I have to get the job!"

Chapter Two

At seven the next morning, Bonnie heard a tap on her door and a quiet voice called, "Bonnie, breakfast in twenty minutes."

Bonnie stretched and smiled. The sun was streaming through the lace curtains, tracing patterns across the rosebuds on the wallpaper. The room was even more attractive in the sunlight. Bonnie hopped from the bed and walked to the window. The night before, she had sat in a wing chair by this same window, trying to concentrate on her book but being distracted by her thoughts. She had peered through the window, lulled by the song of the crickets, but had been unable to see past the branches of a huge tree that sheltered the house.

Now she was pleased to find that her room over-looked a carefully tended herb garden. A breeze stirred the curtains, and even at this hour Bonnie could tell it would be another hot, humid day. Liz had apologized for the lack of air-conditioning, but Bonnie hadn't missed it in this large, airy room. *What a wonderful place to live!* she thought wistfully.

Now she hurried to the bathroom, where she quickly showered and dressed in a sleeveless cotton blouse and a short denim skirt. She wished she had packed shorts and a T-shirt. She pulled her light-brown hair into a ponytail and was ready for the day.

When she had repacked her overnight bag, she carried it downstairs with her and placed it in the front hall. She followed her nose to the kitchen, where Tim stood at the stove scrambling eggs while Liz snuggled in the rocking chair, giving Joshua his breakfast. It was such an intimate scene that Bonnie stood shyly in the doorway for a moment.

Tim, dressed in clean overalls and with his red hair slicked down, grinned at her in welcome.

"Good morning. Sleep well?"

"Like the proverbial log. That's a wonderful room."

"Glad you like it. Liz tells me you may be staying with us for a while."

"I hope so, if you're sure you don't mind."

"Fine with me. I'll like it better than having folks in and out every weekend."

Liz opened her eyes and laughed. "Tim, stop trying to sound like Farmer Brown. Bonnie's got your number. Tim sometimes has trouble being affable to total strangers, Bonnie, so he hides behind his hayseed disguise.''

Tim dumped the eggs onto a yellow platter and brought them to the table with a sheepish grin on his face. He poured coffee into the yellow mugs and passed Bonnie a basket of muffins while Liz burped the baby and put him into his basket. For a moment they all enjoyed the food in silence. Then Liz began to tell Tim her plans for the day, which began with dropping Bonnie at the center by eight o'clock.

''You might as well leave your car at the store and walk back later. I'm going to want to hear how your day went, anyhow.''

''Sounds good to me,'' Bonnie said, helping Liz load the dishwasher and gather up the baby's necessities.

Tim carried the baby out to the station wagon and strapped him into the car seat. He dropped a kiss on the baby's fuzzy head and one on Liz's cheek and with a casual wave to Bonnie and a cheerful ''Good luck,'' he strode off to the blue truck in the driveway.

''What a nice man!'' Bonnie said with a sigh.

Liz looked at her with surprise. ''He is, isn't he? We've been together so long, since our first year in college, I guess I sometimes take him for granted.''

''I hope I can meet someone that nice.''

''No boyfriend back home?'' Liz asked as she pulled onto Route 101.

''Nobody serious.''

"Well, be patient. You never know when the right guy will come along."

Bonnie reached over the seat and ran her fingers through Joshua's feathery hair. "Maybe I'll wait for this guy," she said.

"Long wait," Liz said with a laugh, "and, anyway, I'm not sure I'd approve of such an older woman, no matter how much I liked her. Well, here you are, even a little early."

"Thanks, Liz." Bonnie's smile was strained as she left the car and climbed the steps of the center.

The oak doors were closed this morning, and as she passed into the cheerful foyer, Bonnie paused to listen to the sounds coming from the various rooms of the center. She knew that the door to her right led to the kindergarten classroom, where, in September, the five-year-olds would meet with their teacher. Now the room was being used for arts and crafts, but since New Hampshire conducted no public kindergarten, the room would serve fifteen children in the fall.

Bonnie walked straight ahead and opened the door to the main room, where several small children were finishing breakfast at miniature wooden picnic tables.

"Hi," a little blond boy called out. "Who are you? A teacher or a mother?"

"I'm Bonnie," she said with a smile. "Who are you?"

"I'm Brendan, and he's Miles," the blond answered. "He doesn't talk much."

Bonnie smiled at Miles, who appeared to be under two years old, as he concentrated on chasing the last Cheerio around the remaining milk in his bowl.

"We offer breakfast for those children who can't seem to handle it so early in the morning at home. As it is, some of the families have to wake the children to get them here on time." Kate had appeared at Bonnie's shoulder.

Bonnie followed Kate into the play area, where small groups of children were engaged in various activities under the supervision of two young women. A woman in her late thirties was seated on a mat with a group of two-year-olds around her while she sang nursery rhymes in a soft voice.

"Let me introduce you to our staff. First, Martha Dario." Martha rose from the mat and extended her hand. "Martha spends most of her time with the youngest children. Some of them are under two and miss their mothers. Martha is wonderful at her job. Sometimes she carries the little ones around, and she keeps track of their days. She often writes notes to their moms. We couldn't do without her."

Martha smiled at Bonnie. "Hi, Bonnie, I've heard a lot about you already."

"Martha and I have been here since six-thirty," Kate explained. "I don't usually have to be here that early, but staffing was off this morning, and things were a little crazy."

The other women had left their charges and were waiting to be introduced.

"Bonnie, this is Donna. She's been with us for the summer but will be returning to college in the fall. We hope to see her here on vacations. Right, Donna?"

Donna shrugged in a noncommittal manner and returned to the children.

The other young woman smiled at Bonnie. "I'm Greta. I'm here for the duration. I usually work with the four-year-olds," she said shyly. "They're my favorites."

"Mine, too," Bonnie confided.

"Okay, that's our summer staff, except for our aides. Of course, it all changes when school opens. Now, let's find your children," Kate said briskly. She looked around the main room and then led Bonnie to Greta's group. "I thought I'd find the boys here."

Seated on a mat at Greta's feet were two little boys whose distinctive features were symptomatic of Down's Syndrome. Each held a hand puppet, and Greta was encouraging them in her gentle voice to place the puppets on their chubby hands. Kate placed a hand lightly on the dark hair of the larger boy. "This is Joel, and he's five. He's a very good boy, and he loves fishing and playing ball. Don't you, Joel?"

Joel nodded his head affably. He wiggled his hand into an Ernie puppet and rubbed his snub nose against Ernie's round, red nose.

"This is Freddie, and he's four." Kate indicated the

other boy, who was struggling with the Big Bird hand puppet. "Freddie loves music. Right, Freddie?"

Freddie smiled and thrust a chubby hand in Bonnie's direction. She shook it solemnly, saying, "How do you do, Freddie?"

"Freddie's dad is big on socialization," Kate said. "It's very important to him that Freddie be socially acceptable. We'd just like to get him toilet-trained!"

They left the boys in Greta's care and walked across the large room, pausing here and there to pat a head or redirect an activity. In the other room they found three teenage girls assisting a group of older children with finger paints. The girls smiled cheerfully at Kate and waved blue, yellow, and red fingers at Bonnie in lieu of a handshake.

"These are our summer aides—Cheryl, Jennifer, and Lisa. You'll get to know them all in time. Some of them may decide to stick around the rest of the year. I wish they could stay with us forever—they're invaluable."

The girls giggled and returned to their paints, stealing curious glances at Bonnie.

"Okay. Which one of you is hiding Ethan this time?"

A slim blond girl with braces on her teeth and freckles on her nose blushed slightly and pointed under her chair. Kate bent over to peer under the table. "Come on, Ethan," she said firmly. "Come out from under Jennifer's chair."

Bonnie was surprised to see Kate help a small boy out from under the table. He stood quietly at her side, his head bowed, but his fingers moved quickly, weaving intricate patterns.

"Bonnie, this is Ethan. Ethan, say hello to Bonnie." The child raised his head slowly, and for a moment Bonnie caught a glimpse of startling blue eyes. Then he was gone. Like quicksilver, he darted across the room to the far corner, where he began to spin in wider and wider circles.

Kate nodded at Bonnie. "Autistic. He'll be your biggest challenge."

"What a beautiful child!" Bonnie commented.

"Autistic children are often quite beautiful. No one seems to know why. Maybe it's a compensation for what they miss," Kate said with a rueful smile.

"How old is he?" Bonnie asked as she watched Ethan, fascinated by his quick and erratic movements.

"He's just five. I've had him with me for two years, and he's a constant challenge, but I've become very attached to him. We'll leave him for a moment and let him settle down. Jennifer will keep an eye on him. She's very fond of him."

Kate led Bonnie back to her office. "The other two children you'll work with will be in after lunch. They've been coming half days for the summer, but they'll be here full-time in September. Let me show you the journals we keep for the children."

Kate sat behind her desk while Bonnie returned to

the orange chair. Kate pulled a stack of slim notebooks from a shelf behind her desk and passed them to Bonnie. Each book had a name printed in bold Magic Marker blazoned across the front. Bonnie looked for Ethan's and held it lightly in her hands.

"You can open it," Kate directed.

Bonnie paged through the book, noticing the variety of handwritings and messages recorded. "One of the teachers writes in the book every day, and the book goes home with the child. It's to inform the family what kind of a day the child had, the progress made, or difficulties encountered. As you can see, they're pretty routine messages, but occasionally a little triumph is recorded or a problem discussed."

Bonnie read a few words aloud. "Ethan sat quietly in the circle."

Kate nodded. "A real feat for Ethan. Anyhow, the family is supposed to add their contribution every evening about the time at home and bring the book back in the morning. They're pretty good about it, some better than others, of course. As you can see, Ethan's father is very reliable."

Bonnie flipped through the book and could see that alternate pages held a masculine handwriting. Sometimes there were only a few lines, often a small paragraph, but always the same hand. "Doesn't Ethan's mother ever write in the book?" she asked.

"Ethan's father is a single parent. He's an interesting man. You'll meet him this afternoon when he comes to pick up Ethan. David has full custody of his son, and every Friday night he and Ethan go out for pizza.''

Bonnie and Kate went through the rest of the books. ''These books will be part of your duties, if you take the job,'' Kate said casually.

Bonnie stacked the books neatly. ''May I ask you something?''

''Of course,'' Kate said.

''Why are you giving up this class? You seem to love it so much.''

For a moment Bonnie thought Kate blushed. ''A couple of reasons,'' she replied. ''For one, I've had the class for five years, and I'm suffering a little teacher burnout. We need some new ideas in here, a little creative thinking. Everyone will benefit.''

''And the other reason?'' Bonnie prompted.

Kate rested her chin on her hand. ''The truth is, I'm thinking of having another child.'' A dimple flashed in her cheek. ''It's that darn biological Timex ticking away.'' She rose from her chair hurriedly. ''That's just between you and me. Okay?''

''Of course,'' Bonnie replied, following Kate to the door.

''By the way,'' Kate asked in the doorway, ''how is your sign language? One of your students, Tina, is profoundly deaf and very adept.''

''I've had two semesters of instruction. I think I can keep up.''

"Good. If we hurry, we can catch the end of the circle."

Bonnie followed Kate into the big room. A little thrill of excitement passed through her. Kate had said, "One of your students." It seemed Kate had made up her mind.

Just before they joined the circle, Kate whispered, "I guess you realize the job is yours if you want it."

Bonnie just smiled her answer.

Kate managed to keep Bonnie busy for the rest of the morning. When outdoor playtime arrived at eleven-thirty, Bonnie was happy to go outside into the enclosed yard and watch the children enjoy their free time on the sturdy equipment. She noted that Ethan went straight for the sandbox, where he filled a cup and emptied it over and over. Watching him from the corner of her eye, she rolled a large, colorful ball to Joel and Freddie, who giggled and tumbled in the grass, attempting to kick it back to her.

At noon the aides gathered the children and herded them back inside, where, after many trips to the bathroom and much hand washing, they were ready for lunch. Bonnie helped the girls serve macaroni and cheese, carrot sticks, applesauce, and milk, followed by paper cups of red Jell-o. Wiping up spills and settling small squabbles kept her occupied until Kate emerged from her office to greet a young woman escorting two little girls into the room.

"Hi, girls," Kate called to the children, one of whom wore a hearing aid in each ear. Kate bent to this child and signed, "How are you today, Tina?"

The child's dark eyes lit up as her slender fingers signed an answer. The other girl waited patiently, resting on her walker until Kate tugged gently on her ponytail.

"And you, Pammy?"

"I'm fine, too, Miss Kate. Mommy brought us today."

"I see that, sweetheart. How's it going, Marge?"

"Pretty good. Pammy's having a good summer, but she's looking forward to coming back full-time."

"I'm glad to hear that. Marge, I'd like you to meet someone," she said, leading the woman to Bonnie, who was trying to wipe Jell-o from Ethan's face.

"Marge, this is Bonnie Delaney. Bonnie, this is Marge Dysart, Pammy's mother. She and Tina's mother have been taking turns bringing the girls to the center this summer, but in the fall they'll ride on the bus."

"I'm glad to meet you," Bonnie said.

"Bonnie will be taking the group in September," Kate announced to Marge's surprise.

"You won't be working with Pammy anymore?"

"Not directly. I'm doing the administrative work this year. But I'll be training Bonnie for the rest of the summer, and I'm sure it will work out fine," she said firmly. She led Marge Dysart to the door while Bonnie introduced herself to the little girls.

"There will be some resistance to the change," Kate said casually when she returned, "but don't worry about it."

Bonnie had no doubt that Kate would handle it.

The rest of the afternoon was taken up with naps, Play-Doh, and quiet activities until three o'clock, when the children were again let outside for outdoor play.

"How are you doing?" Martha asked Bonnie as they pushed Joel and Freddie on the swings.

"Okay, I think, but there's a lot to learn," Bonnie replied, glancing toward the sandbox, where Ethan had returned to fill and dump again.

"But you are going to take the job?" Martha asked.

"Oh, yes," Bonnie said with enthusiasm. "Could you just push Freddie for a moment? Pammy seems to be having trouble with her walker in the grass."

Martha smiled as Bonnie hurried to the little girl's side.

When she had escorted Pammy to the jungle gym, Bonnie went to sit beside Ethan in the sandbox, where she tried to interest him in packing sand into a mold. She was so intent on the small boy that she didn't notice Kate's approach until she called her name.

"Bonnie, Ethan's father is here."

Bonnie looked up to see a tall, slender man watching her with a guarded look on his face. He had sun-streaked hair and a lean face with high cheekbones.

As she scrambled to her feet, brushing sand from her hands, she couldn't help noticing that he had the same startling blue eyes as his son.

"David Anderson, this is Bonnie Delaney, Ethan's new teacher. Actually, her title is 'integration facilitator,' but that sounds too stuffy."

David Anderson frowned slightly before extending his hand to Bonnie, who was still scrubbing her palm against her denim skirt.

"It's nice to meet you," Bonnie said with a shy smile.

David's hand was warm and dry in hers, and for a brief moment she was reluctant to let it go. Flustered, she watched a slow smile erase some of the worry lines from his face.

"Kate tells me she has every confidence in you, so I'm sure Ethan will be okay. It's just that he doesn't take well to change. . . ."

"I understand," Bonnie said. "I'll try to make the transition as smooth as possible."

"I'm sure you will." He bent to get Ethan's attention.

Ethan glanced at his father briefly, but his fingers persisted in their repetitive motions. David reached down and scooped up the child, tossing him over his shoulder, limp and unprotesting. "Come on, buddy," he said. "Pizza night."

"Enthusiastic, isn't he?" he said to Bonnie with a grin.

"Bonnie, why don't you go inside with David and give him Ethan's journal? I wrote in it today, but from now on it will be your job."

Bonnie followed David into the building and handed him the small notebook.

"So we will be corresponding," he said lightly, taking the book from her hand.

"It seems so."

"Well, I'll try not to make it too dull," he promised as he carried Ethan out the door.

Bonnie walked to the wide front window, where Jennifer was watching David settle Ethan in his car seat.

"Gorgeous, isn't he?" Jennifer said dramatically.

Bonnie didn't answer, but she had to agree.

Chapter Three

When Bonnie returned to the playground, Kate greeted her with an understanding smile.

"You've had a long day. Why don't you go along now and make your arrangements with Liz about the room? She'll be happy to know you've accepted the job."

"If you're sure you don't need me anymore today."

"No, we're fine. Are you going back to Massachusetts tonight?"

"Yes. I'll have to talk to my folks and pack some of my things. What time should I be here on Monday morning?"

"Why don't you get here about eight-thirty? We still need to work out some details. Oh, by the way, jeans or shorts are fine. We spend so much time on the floor, it's silly to dress."

"Great! I'll see you then," Bonnie replied, and with a wave to the other staff members, she left the center for the short walk to the farm stand.

"Hi, Bonnie," Liz called cheerfully over the tinkle of the bell that announced her entrance into the shop. "Well, how was your day? I assume you have a new job?"

"Yes, I do," Bonnie replied with a triumphant smile, while leaning wearily on the counter.

"I thought so. I called Kate this morning and told her she'd be a fool not to hire you. I hope you've decided to stay with us."

"I'd love to, if you're sure it wouldn't be too much trouble for you."

"On the contrary. It will be easier than having people in and out. Will you be with us for supper tonight?"

"Thank you, but I'd better not. I have to drive back home and pack my things. If I leave now, I can be there by seven. But would it be all right if I come back on Sunday night?"

"Sure, that's fine. Your room should be empty, but if not, there's a pull-out couch downstairs that you can use for one night."

"Hey," Bonnie said suddenly, peering over the top of the counter, "where's Joshua?"

"Oh, Tim's mom took him for a little while. I needed to do some stocking of the shelves, and she loves to get her hands on Binky any chance she can get.''

''That's nice. My mom has a real thing for the grand-children, too. Well, I'd better get going. I'm sure to hit traffic in Nashua again.'' Reluctantly she left the cool, fragrant atmosphere of the store and climbed into her hot car for the trip back home.

Bonnie's parents, though less than enthusiastic, were very understanding and supportive about her new job and the move it entailed. They helped her pack the basic necessities but reminded her that there was no reason why she shouldn't come home every weekend to be with the family. Bonnie assured them that she would come back as often as possible, but in her heart she hoped to make a place for herself in Abbots Hill.

On Sunday afternoon the whole clan gathered as they usually did. Her two married brothers and her sister with their children clustered around the gas grill in the Delaney yard, while her dad cooked hot dogs and ham-burgers and the women dished out salads and baked beans. It was a lovely day, like so many they had enjoyed together, and for a moment Bonnie wondered how much she would miss the comfort and security she had always enjoyed as the youngest, much-loved child of this warm, close-knit family.

''You're doing the right thing, you know,'' a quiet voice said beside her. She turned to find her oldest brother, Kevin, squatting down beside her chair, a soft drink in one hand and a hot dog in the other. She looked into his soft-brown eyes, and tears came into hers.

"It's harder than I thought," she said softly.

"I know, but you should remember that you were the only one of us who didn't go away to college. We all made the break at eighteen, but you have to do it sometime. Mom and Dad really understand that in their hearts."

"I hope so. I don't want to hurt them."

"Don't worry so much, Bunny," he said, using her old nickname. "Dad will be retiring soon, and you know how they plan to travel. Maybe they'll even make that famous trip to Ireland."

Just then, her nephew, Brian, jumped on his father's back, spilling soda all over Bonnie's legs. In the ensuing confusion, she forgot her misgivings and enjoyed the rest of the afternoon.

By seven o'clock, with the old Nova packed to capacity, she was on her way back to Abbots Hill and her new life. In her mind she kept picturing the children who would soon be her responsibility. The two little boys, Joel and Freddie, were so sweet and would be fun to work with, and Pammy was such a bright little girl and quite agile with her walker. She would be easy to integrate with the other children. Tina would be more of a challenge, but Bonnie had packed her textbooks on American Sign Language and would brush up on her skills.

She had to admit that the child who interested her

most was Ethan. From what she had observed in her short time with him, he spoke very seldom, and even then it was mostly a repetition of someone else's words. Bonnie wondered if anyone had ever tried to teach Ethan to sign. She would have to ask Kate.

It would be so exciting if she could accomplish some sort of a breakthrough with Ethan, she thought, and then shook herself mentally for being so incredibly naive. *You're in for a lot of hard work*, she reminded herself, *so don't be looking for miracles*. But she knew Ethan's father would be cooperative. Maybe she could teach him to sign too.

When she thought of David Anderson, she remembered the look on his face when he took Ethan's journal from her hands. She recalled what it felt like to look into those blue eyes, and then, despite her stern reminders to herself, she spent the rest of the drive to New Hampshire picturing David's face.

It was twilight when she pulled her car into the drive of the old farmhouse that would now be her home. She climbed the wooden steps and found Liz seated in a porch swing that squeaked as she rocked Joshua into an uneasy slumber.

"How's he doing?" Bonnie asked softly.

"He's having a bad day," Liz murmured as she rubbed the tiny back. Then she smiled at Bonnie. "But we're glad you're back, and I'm happy to say your room is empty. I didn't get around to making up your bed, but the clean linens are on the dresser. I didn't think you would mind.''

''Of course not. I assume I'll be taking care of my own room in the future, anyway.''

''That would be lovely,'' Liz said with a sigh. ''Tomorrow remind me to show you where the washer and dryer are in the basement.'' She rose wearily from the swing. ''And now, I'm ready for a cup of tea. How about you?''

''I'd love one,'' Bonnie said, following her into the house.

''And some blueberry pie?'' Liz asked over her shoulder.

''Better still,'' Bonnie replied.

The next morning Bonnie awoke to the sound of her own alarm clock. With Tim's help she had brought her suitcases and boxes into the house, and she had half unpacked them before falling into bed and into a sound sleep. During the night a thunderstorm had rolled in, and now a cool, damp breeze was stirring the lace curtains at the window.

When she entered the kitchen, she found only Liz in her chair, with Joshua on her shoulder.

''Tim had to go to the market this morning for produce. He left here at four A.M.,'' Liz volunteered with a yawn.

''Does he do that often?''

"At least twice a week, poor soul. Help yourself to eggs or cereal, whatever you want."

"Cereal is fine," Bonnie answered, taking a bowl from the cupboard. She was relieved that Liz was no longer standing on ceremony; she much preferred to be treated as part of the family. After a breakfast of Raisin Bran and whole-wheat toast with homemade strawberry jelly, she left Liz changing Joshua and drove to the center.

As Bonnie was climbing the steps of the center, she noticed a red truck pulling into the parking lot. Recognizing David and Ethan, she paused on the steps and awaited their approach. She watched Ethan shuffle his feet through the gravel, pausing every few steps to examine a particular stone while his father waited patiently. When they finally reached her, David greeted her cheerfully.

"Good morning," he said. "All ready for your first day?"

"I hope so," Bonnie answered.

"Well, I wish you good luck." David put Ethan's hand in hers. "You might as well take this," he said, handing her Ethan's journal.

He reached over and kissed the boy on the cheek, but Ethan stood stoically, showing no reaction to his father's gesture. Even the small hand that Bonnie held tightly seemed lifeless and indifferent, but at least he hadn't pulled away. David smiled his farewell, and

Bonnie watched him walk to his truck with a lump in her throat.

Bonnie ushered Ethan into the building and handed him over to Jennifer, who was waiting in the doorway, hoping for a glimpse of David.

Bonnie found Kate in her office, furiously trying to catch up with her paperwork.

"Sit a minute while I finish these darn forms. This is the only part of the job that I hate. When I opened the center, I pictured myself spending all my time with the children. What a joke!"

Bonnie slid into the orange chair and opened Ethan's journal while she waited. The entries were quite ordinary, but to Bonnie's surprise there was a small, folded piece of paper clipped to the last page. Carefully she unfolded it and read the contents:

> *I love the little children, and it is not a slight thing when they, who are fresh from God, love us.*
> *Charles Dickens*

Bonnie glanced at Kate, who was still engrossed in her work. She refolded the paper and slipped it into her pocket.

"Okay," Kate said with a sigh, "I'm all set for the moment. Now, about your hours. . . . I think if you work from nine to five, it will be best for your children. Some of them will be here only for school hours. That would be Pammy, Tina, and Joel. Freddie and Ethan are also enrolled in the day-care program, so they're here most of the day. Ethan's dad brings him any time between eight and nine, depending on his schedule for the day, and picks him up about five. David owns a printing business here in town, so he pretty much makes his own hours. If he has an emergency, his mom fills in. Freddie is here at seven-thirty and doesn't get picked up until five, poor lamb. We make sure he has a long nap.''

''Nine to five sounds fine,'' Bonnie said, trying to absorb it all.

''Good. I wrote up a lot of notes for you over the weekend, and of course you'll have access to the children's records, but I want you to work out your own lesson plans. They're your kids now,'' Kate said with her dimpled smile.

''You did tell me I would have an aide. Will she be in today?''

''Oh, yes, Faith will be here any minute. I think you'll like her. She took a few days off last week to help her mother, who just had her twelfth child.'' Kate smiled at Bonnie's look of surprise. ''Faith belongs to the Finnish community. They have a lot in common with the Amish and share many of their values. I think you'll find Faith fascinating.''

''I'm really looking forward to meeting her,'' Bonnie said sincerely.

Bonnie was sitting on the mat with Freddie and Joel

when Kate called her attention to the young woman standing by her side.

"Bonnie, this is Faith Ojela," she said simply.

"Don't get up," a pleasant voice advised her. "I'll join you."

Bonnie extended her hand to the blond woman who sat cross-legged beside her. If Kate hadn't told her that Faith was twenty years old, she wouldn't have been able to guess her age. Faith had a square face, with blond hair pulled back into one long braid. Her complexion was ruddy with good health and devoid of makeup, but her calm manner and the obvious competence of her large, square hands promised a maturity that Bonnie sensed she would soon come to envy.

"I'm happy to meet you," Faith told her as Joel crawled into her lap and rested his head on her shoulder.

"I'll leave you two to get acquainted." Kate gave them a benevolent smile as she retreated to her office.

Bonnie was tongue-tied for a moment. "Tell me about the children," she said desperately.

"That will take days," Faith replied sensibly, "but I'll help you make out a schedule for today."

She rose from the mat in a fluid motion and led Bonnie to a quiet corner. Bonnie followed her gratefully and listened intently while Faith made suggestions for four of the children. When she came to Ethan, she shrugged. "With Ethan we can only hope. Your guess is as good as mine."

Unfortunately, her words proved prophetic. When Ethan was finally pried away from Jennifer and gently encouraged to join the others in the circle, he balked in no uncertain terms and flung himself into a corner of the room.

"Let him be," Faith advised. "We'll try again later."

The other four children were more than happy to sit in the circle and participate in the morning activities.

Bonnie could see Faith watching Ethan from the corner of her eye. She trusted Faith's judgment and so allowed herself to enjoy Pammy's happy smile and Tina's enthusiastic signing when the children sang a morning song.

She was startled when she felt Faith tap her arm. "There he goes," she whispered.

Bonnie jumped to her feet. She ran to the other side of the room, where Ethan was starting to climb a bookcase on the far wall. Faith followed her in a more leisurely fashion. With sure steps the child scaled the shelves, carefully placing his feet among the toys and games stacked there. Bonnie was surprised to notice that Kate and the other teachers didn't even leave the group.

"Shouldn't we stop him?" she asked.

"No," Faith answered simply.

They reached the bookcase just as Ethan placed a small, sneakered foot on the top. He was now ten feet off the ground and poised arms outstretched. For a moment he was totally still, and then he began moving his arms in a flapping motion. Bonnie was frightened. "He's not going to—" she gasped.

"Fly off? No fear of that. He won't fall, either. He's as surefooted as a baby goat."

"What do we do?"

"Wait a few moments until he's calm and then coax him to come down."

"I'll get him down," a small voice piped up at Bonnie's elbow.

"No, you will not," Faith said firmly to Brendan, who had a large ball raised over his head. "Brendan, put that ball down and get back to the circle." She turned the boy around and headed him back to the group.

"Brendan is very enthusiastic. Unfortunately, he views Ethan as a toy caught in a tree and would like to bounce him off."

Bonnie hadn't taken her eyes away from Ethan, so she watched his erratic motions slow down until he was motionless again.

"I'll be right back," Faith said, walking away. When she returned, she held up a cracker and in a calm, deliberate manner called to Ethan in her quiet voice.

It took a few moments for him to notice the cracker, but finally he put one deliberate foot onto a lower shelf and then slowly descended, to stand head bowed before them. Bonnie expelled the breath she had been holding and stifled the urge to hug the child as he accepted the cracker and munched it eagerly.

"Does he do that often?" Bonnie asked.

"Only when he's really upset," Faith replied.

"Because of my being here?"

Faith laid a hand gently on her arm. "Perhaps, but I don't think so. Ethan is very unpredictable. Anything can set him off."

Together they led the child back to the circle, where he settled himself at Jennifer's side with a sigh. His small escapade seemed to have exhausted him or released some unknown tension, because he sat quietly while the other children went on to the art room for a turn at the finger paints.

What will I write in his journal? Bonnie asked herself as she helped Pammy swirl blue paint. *What can I say to Ethan's father?*

As it turned out, no explanation on her part was necessary. The rest of Ethan's day was uneventful, and Kate advised her to relate that in his journal.

When David Anderson arrived to pick up his son, Kate met him at the door and took him quietly aside. "Ethan was climbing again today, David. Anything going on at home?"

David shrugged. "Nothing special. Could be anything, you know that, Kate."

"Well, Bonnie was upset. Of course she thinks it's because of her. I tried to reassure her, but it's her first day."

"Want me to talk to her?"

"It would be a kindness," Kate answered.

David walked across the room to where Bonnie was putting away the hand puppets. "Bonnie?" David smiled into her flushed face.

Startled, she dropped Big Bird onto the floor and was happy to bend over to hide the blush she couldn't control. David bent with her, and his warm hand brushed hers as they both tried to retrieve the yellow bird. Bonnie was so flustered that she almost snatched the puppet from his hands.

"Okay, it's yours," he said with a laugh, raising his hands. "I prefer Ernie myself."

Bonnie turned swiftly and crammed the puppet onto the shelf. "Sorry," she mumbled.

"I just wanted to say a word to you about Ethan's climbing."

Bonnie spun around and tried to compose her face. Before she could speak, David continued, "Don't let it worry you. He does it all the time. Usually it's when he's upset, but anything can set him off. He does it at home too. I had to bolt all the furniture to the floor."

"I thought it might have been my taking the class," Bonnie said.

"I doubt it. More likely something I did on the way to school." He smiled reassuringly. "Try not to let it frighten you. Wait until he climbs to the top of the jungle gym outside."

"I can't wait," Bonnie replied, trying to smile in return.

Just then Kate joined them, leading Ethan by the hand, and Bonnie excused herself to get the journal. After David and Ethan were gone, she wondered—if Kate had not come along, would she have had the courage to mention the note she had found in the book that morning? She decided that she would not have, even if they had been alone. *Am I going to keep making a fool of myself with this man? Oh, please, I hope not,* she thought.

Chapter Four

The rest of the summer passed swiftly for Bonnie. With some difficulty she convinced her parents that she would be perfectly safe and happy staying in Abbots Hill for most weekends but agreed to spend at least one weekend a month visiting her family in Massachusetts. Kate was an excellent teacher, and soon Bonnie was quite comfortable with her group, although Ethan continued to present a challenge. Bonnie and Faith made an efficient team and were able to work together smoothly, while Faith continued to surprise Bonnie with the differences in their cultures and backgrounds.

One day when Faith was having difficulty understanding Tina's combination of halting speech and rapid signing, Bonnie laughed and said, ''Faith, she's getting ahead of you. Why don't you take a course in sign language?''

Faith shook her head. ''That wouldn't be possible.''

''Why not? Is it transportation? I'm thinking of taking a course toward my master's degree this September. Maybe you could ride with me.''

''No, it's not that. Education for women is not encouraged in my family.''

Bonnie was shocked. ''Do you mean you wouldn't be permitted to go to school?''

''It's not forbidden; it's just not encouraged,'' Faith replied, effectively closing the subject.

But Bonnie wasn't satisfied. ''Suppose I bring in my American Sign Language books. Would that help?''

''That would be wonderful,'' Faith answered with her luminous smile.

''By the way,'' Bonnie asked, ''did Kate ever try to teach Ethan to sign?''

''We both tried a few times, but we weren't very successful. As you know, Ethan usually repeats what's said to him but never uses personal pronouns. It makes his speech very confusing. We hoped to teach him the basic signs for when he's hungry or needs to use the bathroom, but when he refuses to make eye contact, it's very difficult.''

''Yes, I can see that,'' Bonnie agreed, ''but maybe if we persist. . . .''

''I'm willing. It will be good practice, so Tina won't

be so frustrated with me,'' Faith said with a laugh. ''You might want to mention it to his dad,'' Faith added. ''He likes to be kept up-to-date.''

Bonnie had no intention of making a fool of herself again with David Anderson. She decided to put a note in Ethan's journal about their plans. Since it was a Friday, she knew he would be arriving at five sharp to take Ethan for their pizza night, so she could hand him the journal and leave.

Her plan started out fine. She met David at the door, handed him the journal, smiled sweetly, and ran for her car. David stood for a moment on the steps, looking confused by her hurried departure, but then he led Ethan to the truck and placed him in his seat. For a moment he paused and glanced at the journal.

In the meantime Bonnie was trying in vain to start her car, but when she turned the key in the ignition, the car just made grinding noises. Finally, after several tries, it coughed into life, just as she heard a voice at her window. She turned to find David at her side. ''Your battery is low. You'd better get it charged,'' he advised.

''Thank you. I'm sure you're right,'' she answered.

''Oh, by the way, I read your note in the journal about teaching Ethan to sign. It's fine with me. The last time Kate tried, I took a short course at the library, and I think I still remember the basics. Maybe you could help me brush up?''

''I'd be happy to,'' Bonnie answered primly.

"Okay, then, I'll see you. I'd better get back to Ethan," David said, walking off.

When he was out of sight, Bonnie rested her head on the steering wheel and moaned, "I'd be happy to," mimicking herself. She decided to surprise her mother and go home to spend some time with her family, especially since she would miss the annual Labor Day picnic.

On Monday morning, after a relaxing weekend, Bonnie was surprised to find a note clipped to the last page of Ethan's journal. Carefully she unfolded it and found the first stanza of a poem:

There was a child went forth every day,
And the first object he look'd upon, that object he
*   became,*
And that object became part of him for the day or a
*   certain part of the day,*
Or for many years or stretching cycles of years.
*   Leaves of Grass*

It was a poem she was familiar with and which she loved. But why did he include it now, after all these weeks? That night she found the poem by Walt Whitman in a collection she had brought from home and copied the second stanza on a piece of stationery and clipped it to the journal.

There were no more notes that week, and since Jennifer always hustled Ethan to his father's side in order to spend a few moments in David's presence, Bonnie didn't see David until Friday night, when they again left the center together. For a moment Bonnie thought David intended to speak to her, but Ethan was being particularly difficult, and David seemed preoccupied with the child.

Bonnie walked slowly to her car while David strapped Ethan into his seat. David was walking around the back of the truck when she inserted the key into the ignition and tried to start her car. A familiar grinding sound reached her ears, and she realized she had never bothered about the battery. This time the engine refused to turn over at all.

She smiled ruefully at the man at her window. "I guess my car doesn't like Friday nights," she said.

"No, I guess you didn't charge the battery," David replied. "Don't worry. I've got jumper cables in the truck."

He left, and in a moment she could hear the truck start, and he was soon pulling it up, nose to nose with the Nova. She released the hood and got out of the car to stand beside him in the gravel. She could see Ethan watching them through the car window, but when she waved to him, he turned away.

David deftly put the cables in place and then started the truck. Within a few minutes he had the Nova running again, although roughly.

"I'd better follow you home," he advised. "We don't want you stuck on that back road."

Bonnie smiled to herself as she drove slowly down Route 101 past the farm stand and onto the dirt road that led to the MacCreadys'. Even if the car did fail here, she would be less than a half a mile from home. She didn't plan to mention that to David. When they reached the farmhouse, she parked in her usual spot and walked back to the truck, where David was leaning out of the truck window.

"You'd better bring it into the garage tomorrow for a slow charge," he said.

"I will," she promised. "Thanks so much for helping me out," she added, starting to walk away.

"Hey, wait a minute." To her surprise, David hopped down from the truck and approached her. "Would you like to come for pizza with Ethan and me?"

"I'd love to," she answered.

"Nothing fancy. We just go into town to Mario's."

"That's fine, but do you mind if I change my shirt?" She indicated the Jell-o and juice stains that adorned her T-shirt.

"Okay by me. And one other thing . . . we'll have to take your car. There are only two seat belts in the truck."

Bonnie ran into the house and called Liz's name from the foyer.

"In the kitchen," came the reply.

"Liz," she said breathlessly, "I won't be here for dinner. I'm going out for pizza with David Anderson."

Liz raised one eyebrow in surprise.

"Don't look like that. It's no big deal. I'm just going to change my shirt." Within minutes she was back downstairs, dressed in a blue cotton dress and white sandals. Her hair shone from brushing and was pulled back with a silver barrette.

Liz was waiting at the foot of the stairs with Joshua on her shoulder.

"Just changed your shirt, I see."

"Oh, Liz, my shorts had Play-Doh on them," Bonnie explained.

"Have a good time and don't be late."

"Thanks, Mom," Bonnie said with a grin.

When Bonnie reached her car, she saw that David had transferred Ethan's booster seat to the back of the Nova, and he was waiting for her in the passenger seat.

"Are you sure my car will make it?" she asked as she slipped into the driver's seat.

"I think so. We'll take it for a run after dinner if you're worried. Do you know how to get to Mario's?" he asked.

"Yes, I've been there with Liz and Tim."

"Good. I always call ahead and order our pizza. Ethan doesn't wait well. I hope you like pepperoni; it's his favorite."

"That's fine with me," she said, driving toward downtown Abbots Hill.

When they reached the restaurant, the owner greeted them with enthusiasm. He was a tall, balding man with a booming voice and friendly black eyes. "David, how nice to see you with such a pretty lady!"

David only laughed while Bonnie blushed.

"How about whipping up a small antipasto while we're waiting for the pizza?" he said before leading Bonnie to a booth.

Within minutes Mario presented the antipasto with a flourish and a wink. While Bonnie and David enjoyed the assorted greens, peppers, and cheeses, Ethan removed the black olives and arranged them in circles on the table.

"I hope you don't mind," David remarked, nodding in Ethan's direction.

"I eat with Ethan every day," Bonnie said simply.

When the pizza arrived, David placed a slice on Ethan's dish. He promptly removed the pepperoni slices one by one and formed a pattern on the edge of his plate; then he began to eat the rest of his pizza.

"I thought you said he liked pepperoni?" Bonnie remarked.

"I said it was his favorite. I didn't say he ate it."

For some reason this struck Bonnie as extremely funny, and her laugh was so infectious that David soon joined her, while Mario smiled on them benevolently. From that moment Bonnie's nervousness abated, and she was able to enjoy David's company. She found him self-deprecating and amusing. When they had done justice to the pizza, David suggested that they take the car for a short run and then stop for an ice-cream cone. Bonnie was quick to agree.

When they arrived back at the farmhouse, David moved Ethan to the truck and then walked Bonnie to the door. He stood for a moment looking down at her and then smiled. "Did I tell you how pretty you look in that dress, Bonnie?"

"No, sir, you did not."

"Well, you do. Prettiest schoolmarm we ever had." He bent down and gently kissed her lips, and then he turned away.

As he reached the bottom step, Bonnie called out, "David, why did you put that poem in the journal?"

He turned, and for a moment Bonnie thought he looked a little flustered, but he recovered quickly. "To get your attention, of course," he said.

Bonnie entered the house in a daze. "That you?" Liz called from the family room.

"Who else?" Bonnie walked through the formal living room reserved for the paying guests and then through the cheerful dining room, where the table was already set for morning breakfast.

"Well, I don't have to ask you how it went. I just have to look at you," Liz commented while Tim buried his face in his book.

"Do we have guests this weekend? I see the table is set," Bonnie said.

"Yes, we do, and don't change the subject," Liz told her.

"You weren't expecting anyone, were you?"

"No, they were drive-ins. They're checking the area for places to stay during the hunting season. Two middle-aged men, very macho. Be glad you don't have to share the bathroom with them; they look lecherous."

"What a thing to say!" Tim commented. "Liz doesn't approve of hunting. She's a city girl and gets into the whole Bambi-killer thing," he added.

"I'm afraid I agree," Bonnie said. "I'll stay out of their way in the morning, if I can. Where are they now?"

"Out for dinner. Now stop stalling and tell us about your date."

"It wasn't a date, not really."

"Oh, Liz, let her be. Stop teasing."

"Okay, you're right," Liz admitted. "But seriously, Bonnie, how much do you know about David and his ex-wife, Caroline?"

"Not very much. Kate mentioned that he's a single parent, and Jennifer, who has this enormous crush on him, told me that his wife left him when Ethan was two, right after he was diagnosed as autistic."

"David is a straight guy, Liz. He'll tell her the story when he wants her to know," Tim said flatly.

"Isn't that just like a man! As if they don't gossip their heads off, given half a chance. I wouldn't tell Bonnie anything that wasn't common knowledge," she defended herself.

"In that case, I'm going to check on Binky," Tim said as he left the room.

"Male bonding," Liz said with a grin. "Look, Bonnie, I just don't want you to get hurt. David had a tough time with Caroline, and I think he's still hurting from the experience. It was a classic case; they married very young, and Caroline had expectations that he couldn't meet. Then along came Ethan. He couldn't have been a more difficult baby. You know how hard it is to diagnose autism? In the meantime they were blaming themselves and each other. By the time they knew for sure what the problem was, Caroline was exhausted. She's a beautiful girl, but everyone spoiled her—her family, even David. When she heard the uncertain prognosis, she just couldn't take it. She left, moved to Boston, and gave complete custody to David."

"How in the world did he manage?"

"His mom helped out for the first year until Kate took Ethan at the center. Helen Anderson is still a big help if Ethan is sick or David needs a break, but he rarely takes advantage of her. He has an older sister, too, but she has children of her own and for some reason is afraid of Ethan and won't let him near her kids."

Bonnie shook her head in distress.

"I'm telling you all this so you'll understand what motivates David. He'll never give up on that child, and I'm not sure he has room in his life or his heart—''

"Liz, we just went for pizza."

"Yes, well, you say that, but I recognized the look on your face when you came in. I saw it in my mirror the first time Tim kissed me good night."

When Tim returned with Joshua on his shoulder, Bonnie excused herself and went to bed.

The next morning Bonnie awoke to the smell of pumpkin-nut muffins, and despite her resolution to avoid the hunters, she couldn't resist the temptation of fresh perked coffee. She dressed hurriedly in jeans and a sweatshirt and joined the others in the dining room. The guests turned out to be two businessmen who enjoyed an occasional weekend in the woods and who, far from being lecherous, were charming and almost courtly in their manner.

While Bonnie was helping Liz clear the table, she sensed an awkwardness in Liz that distressed her. Once in the kitchen, Liz turned to her with a troubled expression. "I'm sorry about last night, Bonnie. Tim says I was way out of line."

Bonnie was quick to reassure her friend. "Not at all, Liz. I knew you were just concerned for me. The only thing is. . . ." She paused.

Liz turned from the sink. "Oh, dear, Tim was right, you are upset with me."

"No, no, I'm not. I just got the feeling that you thought I wasn't good for David or not good enough."

"That's not it at all," Liz assured her. "I just think David has had so much sorrow already and such a tough time. . . ."

"And I'm just a kid," Bonnie said.

"No, Bonnie, you're not a kid. It's just that— Oh, I don't know what I mean. I just don't want you to get hurt. As far as I know, you're the first woman David has shown any interest in at all since Caroline left. Maybe he is ready for a relationship."

Whatever Liz would say after that would be lost to Bonnie. All she could remember was that she was the first woman to interest David since Caroline.

On Monday morning Bonnie opened Ethan's journal with trembling fingers. Would there be a poem today, and what would it say? Clipped to the last page, she found:

She was a phantom of delight
When first she gleam'd upon my sight;
A lovely apparition, sent
To be a moment's ornament;
Her eyes as stars of twilight fair;
Like Twilight's, too, her dusky hair;
But all things else about her drawn
From May-time and the cheerful dawn;
A dancing shape, an image gay,
To haunt, to startle, and waylay.

Wordsworth

Bonnie ran to the bathroom, where she read the poem again and then tucked it securely into the pocket of her shorts. She splashed cold water on her face and stood for a moment at the sink, trying to compose her face. "Really, Bonnie," she said to herself, "if you can't control that silly blushing, you might at least get that foolish grin off your face."

The door swung open, and a small voice asked, "Who you talking to, Miss Bonnie?" Brendan looked around the bathroom curiously.

"Just talking to myself, Brendan."

The child nodded sagely. "Could talk to me," he said wistfully.

"Well, when you're finished in the bathroom, you come and find me, and we'll have a chat," she promised, leaving the facilities to him.

Bonnie walked through the main room looking for Faith and soon found her sitting with Tina and Pammy, while Freddie and Joel pounded the Play-Doh into submission. "We were waiting for you. Did you have something special in mind for this morning?"

"I'd like the children to join the circle today. Where is Ethan, by the way?"

"He's hiding with Jennifer again. He's not too pleased with me."

"Anything I should know about?"

"No, just the usual battle over keeping his sneakers on."

"Well, see if you can retrieve him while I find Brendan. I promised him some time this morning."

"Brendan?"

"We met in the bathroom, and he seemed a little forlorn."

"He often is," Faith said sadly. "Bring him along; we can spoil him a little."

Martha was surprised at Bonnie's request to steal Brendan for the morning, but the child had a wonderful time with Freddie and Joel, trying out all the physical therapy equipment. By lunchtime he was worn out and glad to return to his own small group.

"That was fun, having Brendan with us," Pammy said.

"It was," Bonnie agreed. "Maybe we should borrow a three-year-old every now and then. It perked everyone up."

"Not Ethan," Faith observed, pointing out to Bonnie that Ethan had retreated to a corner and was spinning furiously.

Bonnie sighed. "Maybe a little one-on-one would help. If you can manage the others, I'll spend some time alone with him."

"Sure, that's a good idea," Faith replied with a smile. "You'll have better luck if you let him take off his sneakers," she advised.

The rest of the week went fairly well, and on Friday morning Bonnie found a note clipped to Ethan's journal that said, *Sausage pizza tonight. Will you join us?*

Bonnie had finished her paperwork and was ready to leave promptly at five. She was waiting in her car when David approached her. ''I hope you're coming,'' he said.

''I'd love to, but I'll have to change.'' She indicated her rumpled shorts.

''Sure—we'll follow you home.'' He turned and waved to Jennifer, who was watching from the window.

On the way to Mario's, Bonnie asked curiously, ''Are we really having sausage pizza? I thought pepperoni was the favorite.''

''Well, it occurred to me that I was thoroughly sick of pepperoni, and since sausage is also round. . . .''

''Good thinking,'' Bonnie commended him. ''I only hope you're right.''

''Are you doubting my brilliance?'' he asked as she pulled into the parking lot.

''Far be it from me,'' she answered as they swung Ethan between them on their way to the restaurant. Once inside, they greeted Mario and made their way to a booth in the back.

''Mario's really nice, isn't he?'' Bonnie said.

''I'll tell you something funny about him,'' David replied. ''His name is not Mario.''

''It's not?'' she asked, reaching for Ethan, who was trying to slip under the table.

"No, and I don't know what it is. You see, this place has been called Mario's for twenty years. This owner bought it about five years ago, and everyone just began calling him Mario too."

"But that's strange. Doesn't he mind?"

"We'll ask him," David said as the owner placed their antipasto before them.

"Mario, a quick question. I've been telling Bonnie that your name is not Mario. Does it bother you that no one uses your real name?"

The man leaned over the table and whispered, "Don't tell a soul, but I like Mario better. My real name is Hugo."

Bonnie stifled a giggle. "Our lips are sealed," she promised. When Mario had left, she said to David, "That's funny, I always thought someone's personality was tied up in his name."

"I think that's true, so I guess our Mario wanted a change. But what about you? How did you get your name?"

"Oh, that's an old family story."

"Tell me. I'd really like to hear."

She looked into David's intense blue eyes. "I'm not even sure it's true, but my dad says that when I was born, my mother wanted to call me Colleen, but my grandfather, who had originally come from Scotland, took one look at me in the nursery and said, 'Now there's a wee bonnie lass,' and the rest is history."

David's lean hand closed over hers on the shiny table top. "I like that story. If it isn't true, it should be."

Bonnie was saved from having to reply by the arrival of the sausage pizza, which, to their relief, Ethan accepted as a reasonable substitute for the favored pepperoni. After they had finished eating, David suggested a ride to nearby Temple Mountain, where he pointed out the ski lifts and offered to teach Bonnie to ski that winter. He promised to bring her back some Saturday afternoon to ride the lift.

When they arrived back at the farmhouse, Bonnie helped David settle the sleeping Ethan in his car seat. They lingered for a moment on the steps, where David gently took her into his arms and whispered softly against her hair, "She was a phantom of delight."

"David, that poem is beautiful," she murmured.

"It suits you," he replied, and then he was gone.

Chapter Five

O_n Labor Day, Bonnie reported to work at nine o'clock, as usual, to find only Kate and Jennifer staffing the center.

"Not many children today," Kate explained. "Most of the parents have the day off, but there are always a few, mostly single parents who still need our services. It will give you a chance to get to know some of the other children."

Bonnie smiled at the small group of children who stood clustered about Jennifer. They seemed confused to be so few, and some were on the verge of tears. Bonnie singled out a small blond girl whose blue eyes were moist and whose chin quivered.

"Hi there. You're Emily, aren't you?"

The child's ponytail bobbed as she nodded.

"Emily's dad is the police chief in Abbots Hill, and

her mom is the dispatcher, so they're both working today,'' Jennifer explained.

"Well, then," Bonnie said, taking Emily's hand, "we'll have some fun today."

"Me too," Brendan piped up, attaching himself to Bonnie's leg.

"You too," Bonnie agreed, leading the children to the play table.

"Brendan's mother works at McDonald's, so he'll be here all day," Jennifer volunteered. "By the way, did Kate tell you we can only let Brendan go home with his mother or his grandmother?" she whispered.

"Why is that?"

"I'm not sure. You'd better check with Kate."

"Mind if I do that now?" Bonnie asked.

"Sure, go ahead," Jennifer replied, spreading Play-Doh on the table.

"I'll be right back," Bonnie told Emily and Brendan, who had grabbed handfuls of Play-Doh and were pounding it happily.

Bonnie tapped on Kate's office door. "I hate to interrupt your paperwork," she said with a grin, "but do you have a minute?"

"Sure, do you have a problem?"

"No, not really, but Jennifer just mentioned something about releasing Brendan only to certain people?"

Kate frowned and pushed back her chair. She fished through a stack of papers on her desk until she came up with a short list. "I probably should have discussed this with you before, but you're not usually here when these children leave.'' She passed the list to Bonnie, who read through it quickly.

''These children can only be released to the people listed, for various reasons, mostly custody problems. In Brendan's case, there's a court order preventing his father from even seeing him.''

''What happens if he turns up here?''

''We call the police,'' Kate answered simply.

''Have you ever had to deal with a situation like that?''

''Several times. It's always a mess. As you can see from the list, we have a mother who is not allowed to take her child. In her case we occasionally let her visit her child here, but it's painful. Fortunately there are only a few, and we deal with them the best we can. The important thing is to protect the children. We have one advantage—the chief of police is Emily's father, and he's very responsive.''

Sobered by the conversation, Bonnie excused herself to return to Jennifer and the children. They passed a quiet morning playing outside while Kate caught up with her paperwork for the state. They had just served lunch when they were surprised to see Martha Dario coming through the door.

''Hi, Martha, what brings you back here today?'' Kate asked.

''Boredom, to tell the truth. Dick went off to play golf, and there I was alone, so I thought I'd come in and relieve you so you could go to the parade with your family.''

''What a nice idea! Thank you,'' Kate said. ''But are you sure you wouldn't rather have the time to yourself?''

''I had the whole morning, and now I'd rather be with the kids. You go ahead and enjoy the day.''

''I sure will. Let me just call Mark and tell him I'm on my way. Bonnie, why don't you come along? I'd like you to meet Mark and the kids, and I think you would enjoy our little parade.''

''If it's all right with Martha, I'd love to.''

''Fine by me. Jennifer and I can hold down the fort.''

Within minutes Kate and Bonnie were on their way to Kate's house, a short drive away.

''Shouldn't I have brought my car? Surely you won't have room for me and all the kids.''

''No problem. We have a mini-van. We need it to transport Ben in his wheelchair, so the more the merrier,'' Kate said as she pulled into the driveway of a colonial house. ''Come on in,'' she invited. ''The parade doesn't start until one-thirty, so we have time to get the kids ready.''

Bonnie followed Kate to the back deck and through the sliding-glass doors into a large blue-and-white kitchen.

''I'm home,'' Kate called. ''Where is everyone?''

''Upstairs,'' came a masculine voice, quickly followed by a clattering on the stairs. Two small children erupted into the room and threw themselves at their mother. When Kate had disentangled herself from her offspring, she presented them to Bonnie.

"Bonnie, this is Sarah," she said, indicating a slender eight-year-old who had her mother's mass of curly hair and dimpled smile. "And this is Steven." The ten-year-old boy had dark hair, dark eyes, and a serious demeanor. "Children, this is Bonnie, the new teacher at the center." The children smiled their hellos and then clamored around their mother, demanding to know when they were leaving for the parade.

"Is Ben ready to go?" Kate asked.

"Almost. Daddy's getting his overalls on now," Sarah announced. "Ben has a wheelchair," the little girl told Bonnie.

"I know that," Bonnie said solemnly.

"I get to push him sometimes, if I'm very, very careful," Steven told her.

"But not today," his sister told him scornfully. "Daddy said not at the parade."

"No," his mother agreed, "not today." She tousled the boy's hair affectionately. "Steven gets a little rambunctious sometimes, but we feel it does Ben good, most of the time." She turned to greet her husband, who was carrying a small, fragile child. "Mark, this is Bonnie Delaney."

"Hello, Bonnie, I'm glad to meet you. I've heard all sorts of good things about you," Mark said.

"Hello, Mark. That's nice to hear." Bonnie extended her hand to a tall, dark-haired man with intelligent brown eyes and an easy smile. "And this must be Ben," she continued, taking his tiny hand in hers. Ben's heart-shaped face was wreathed in a smile of greeting, and his dark eyes showed the same bright gleam as his dad's.

"Who's ready to go?" Mark asked as he strapped Ben into his wheelchair.

"We are!" the children chorused.

"Can I push Ben down the ramp?" Steven asked hopefully.

"You're kidding," Mark said with a laugh. "Last time you did, he ended up in the woods."

"Hope springs eternal," Kate said, hustling the children out the door.

The children entertained Bonnie on the ride downtown, and when they arrived at Main Street, they found most of the small town assembled with chairs, coolers, and flags. Bonnie was enjoying herself thoroughly when halfway down the block she noticed a familiar figure.

David was standing at the curb, with Ethan perched on his shoulders. Beside him was an older woman who Bonnie assumed was David's mother. Following Bonnie's glance, Kate said, "There's David. Why don't you walk down and say hello? Take Ben with you. He and Ethan are old friends."

Bonnie carefully pushed Ben's wheelchair through the crowd, and when she reached David's side, he greeted her with a warm smile and introduced her to his mother. Helen Anderson shook her hand cordially but couldn't hide her curiosity as she examined Bonnie. David placed Ethan on the ground and led him to Ben's wheelchair.

"Hi, Ethan," Ben said in his precise tones. "Do you want to see the parade?"

"You want to see the parade?" Ethan replied in a monotone.

Ben laughed. "Yes, Ethan, I want to see the parade. Does Ethan want to see it?"

"Ethan wants to see it."

Bonnie looked at David in surprise.

"Ben is one of the few people he talks to. He'll even let Ben touch him sometimes," he told her.

Ethan moved closer to the wheelchair and rested his hand on the arm, while Ben slowly told him about the clowns in the parade. They could hear the first band coming down the block.

"We'd better get Ben back to his family," David said. "I'll walk back with you," he added, turning the chair.

They made slow progress down the street, weaving in and out of the crowd. When they reached the Hollanders, David shook Mark's hand and exchanged a few words with Kate. The band was getting closer, and the children were tugging their parents to the curb when David turned to Bonnie.

"I don't know if Ethan will tolerate the noise, especially when the fire engines hit their sirens, so I'd better get out of this crowd." He touched her hand gently. "Will you join us again on Friday night?"

"I'd love to," Bonnie answered as his fingers pressed hers.

"Good. I'll see you then. Have a good week." He lifted Ethan back to his shoulders and wended his way through the crowd. Bonnie watched him go with a faint smile on her lips. Kate's voice in her ear roused her from her bemused state.

"Jennifer told me you were dating David," she said. "She watches his every move."

"I hope she doesn't mind. I know how she feels about him."

"Jennifer? No, not at all. I heard her telling one of the other girls that she would go out with him in a minute if he weren't so old!"

"That's a relief," Bonnie said with a laugh.

Just then the fire engines arrived with sirens blasting and saved her from Kate's opinion on the situation, but she knew it was only a postponement. It was obvious she would have no secrets from the staff of the center.

Bonnie and Faith devoted the next week to teaching Ethan the rudiments of American Sign Language. By Thursday their combined efforts had resulted only in Ethan's managing to indicate his need for a drink or his desire for a cookie. But at least it was progress of a sort even if most of the time Tina was reduced to fits of giggles.

Friday was a lovely fall day, and Bonnie allowed herself the luxury of looking forward to her date with David. She had carefully avoided the subject with Kate, who was sensitive enough to respect Bonnie's feelings. The day seemed to drag by, and Bonnie was delighted when lunch and naps were finally over and she could take the children out to play.

Once outside, Ethan headed for the sandbox and began to fill a pail. Faith sat beside him and encouraged him to learn the sign for ''sand.'' Bonnie, who was sitting on the steps with Pammy, idly watched them until Faith placed a hand gently on Ethan's cheek to direct his attention. It was a gesture they often used with Ethan, but this time, for some reason, he could not tolerate it. He jumped to his feet and ran to the jungle gym. Faith rose slowly and followed him with no show of alarm.

Bonnie had turned back to the little girl when she heard Faith call her name. She looked up to see that Ethan had climbed to the top of the structure and was standing on a crossbar ten feet above the ground. Bonnie opened the door of the center and called Kate's name and then walked across the yard to stand beside Faith.

''Has he done this before?'' Bonnie asked softly.

''Yes, he has, but it still scares me,'' she replied. ''He won't fall, but we may need some crackers.''

Within moments Kate was beside them, the cracker box in her hand. "I looked out the window," she explained. "You call him, Bonnie."

"Ethan," Bonnie called with a catch in her throat.

"More authority," Kate advised. "Hold up the cracker box."

"Ethan," Bonnie called firmly.

The child balanced on his toes, flapping his arms.

"Come have a cracker," Bonnie suggested.

Ethan continued to ignore them and raised his face to the breeze. The other teachers began to gather the children and lead them back into the building. Kate spoke a few words to Martha, but Faith and Bonnie didn't take their eyes off Ethan. Suddenly they heard Martha call out sharply, "Brendan, come back!"

There was a sudden rush beside them as Brendan ran past them, a soccer ball in his hands. Martha was close on his heels as he shouted, "I'll get him down," and tossed the ball into the air. The ball rose in Ethan's direction, and as Bonnie watched in horror, it glanced off Ethan's shoulder. For a moment the boy seemed poised in air, and then he was plummeting to the ground.

Bonnie reached out to break his fall as he somersaulted toward her and barely managed to deflect his small body before it hit the ground. Bonnie was on her knees in the grass, with Ethan wailing in fright and frustration beside her, when Kate dropped to the ground and ran her hands over Ethan's arms and legs.

Ethan rose shakily to his feet, howling in fear at the sight of the blood dripping from his face. "He's split his chin," Kate announced, examining the boy's face. "Faith, get the ice pack. Bonnie, you stay with him while I call his father and his doctor."

Bonnie sat down in the grass and wrapped the hysterical child in her arms. She knew he would take no comfort from her embrace, but it was necessary to confine him for his own protection. When Faith returned with the ice pack, it took both of their efforts to restrain Ethan and place the compress on his bleeding chin.

"David's on his way. Good thing he was in the plant. Dr. La Rue said to bring Ethan to his office; it's less frightening than the hospital. You'll have to go with David, Bonnie; he'd never manage on his own." Kate was breathless but calm.

Ethan was still struggling in Bonnie's arms when David strode across the play yard. He removed the pack from his son's face and took a quick look at his bleeding chin.

"It doesn't look too deep, but we'll let the doctor decide if he needs stitches. Are you coming with me, Bonnie?" he asked, lifting the child from her arms. For a moment Ethan was quiet in David's arms.

When she nodded her reply, he hurried across the yard with Bonnie in his wake. "We'll take your car," he announced.

"The keys are on the dashboard," Bonnie said, hurrying to keep up. Once at the car, David slipped into the driver's seat after strapping Bonnie and Ethan into one seat belt. She wrapped her arms firmly around the shaking child, who was no longer screaming but was making a keening sound that was as unnerving as his shrieks had been.

"That will have to do. It's a short ride," David said grimly.

"David, I'm sorry. . . ."

"Not your fault; forget it," he said shortly, but then he smiled wryly and touched her shoulder gently. "It's okay, really. Don't worry."

Once at the doctor's office, they were ushered immediately to an examining room, where an elderly man with bushy white eyebrows and a bristly moustache joined them.

He nodded briefly to Bonnie and then addressed David. "Put him on the table, Dave, and let me get a look at that." He bent over the moaning child and gently examined his chin. "Not too bad," he announced, "but he'll need a few stitches." He gave some directions to his waiting nurse and then said to David, "What do you say, Dave? Shall we skip the novocaine?" Catching Bonnie's expression, he turned to her. "Don't look at me like that, miss. Who are you, anyhow?"

"I'm Bonnie Delaney, Ethan's teacher."

"Well, Miss Delaney, I know what you were thinking, but you're wrong. I was not implying that Ethan does not feel pain like any other kid. The problem is, Ethan has an intense fear of needles, and if we can manage without one, we'll have a much easier time.''

''Doc's right, Bonnie,'' David said, stroking Ethan's arms soothingly.

''Okay, let's see how it goes,'' the doctor suggested. ''Dave, you're going to have to hold him down. I hate to use the straps on him. My nurse will hold his head steady, and you, Miss Delaney, will be in charge of his feet. Can you handle that?''

Bonnie nodded and positioned herself at the foot of the table, while the nurse grasped Ethan's head and pulled it back to allow Dr. La Rue to reach his chin. As soon as the doctor approached Ethan with instruments in his hands, the child went into a blind panic. Bonnie found herself grasping his tiny ankles with all her strength while David pressed his entire upper body across the child. As Ethan arched his body against their hands, the nurse calmly held his head while the doctor deftly placed the stitches in his chin.

Suddenly Ethan went limp from exhaustion. Bonnie relaxed her grip on his sneakered feet and leaned forward to David. She could feel his breath on her cheek as they hovered over Ethan. The intimacy of the moment moved her, and it was as if there were no one else in the room but the two of them. David's eyes looked into hers, and she knew he felt it too.

Then Dr. La Rue broke the spell. ''All set here, folks. Don't think he'll even have a scar. Poor little guy will probably sleep for a while. If he's restless tonight, give him some Tylenol, Dave. I'd like to see him around the middle of next week, and we'll get those stitches out.''

David thanked Dr. La Rue and gathered the limp child in his arms. Once in the car, they strapped him into the backseat, where he rested his pale face against the seat, his eyes mere slits, his breathing labored and shallow.

"Is he all right?" Bonnie asked anxiously.

"I think so. He'll sleep for a while now," David replied. He drove slowly back to the school, with Bonnie silent beside him. When they arrived there, Bonnie slipped from her seat.

"Don't move him, please. Take him home in my car. You can bring it back later, or I can catch a ride with Liz," she said.

"Thank you; that's a good idea." David's voice was weary, and Bonnie's heart went out to him. "I'll bring your car back to you as soon as I get him settled."

Bonnie watched David drive away and then slowly climbed the steps of the center. Most of the children had left, but the staff was waiting for her return. "How is he?" Jennifer greeted her anxiously.

Bonnie slumped on to a beanbag chair and gave her report. When she had finished, Kate smiled sympathetically. "Why don't you go along home? If nothing else, you could use a shower."

Bonnie looked down for the first time at her blood-stained shirt and jeans. She felt too exhausted to move.

"I don't have my car," she said listlessly. "David took it."

"I'll drive you home," Martha volunteered.

"Oh, Martha, thanks, but I think I'll wait here for David. I'm sure he'll bring back my car or at least call."

"If that's what you want." Martha shrugged.

"Stay put," Kate told Bonnie. "I'm going to put the kettle on and make you some tea."

Bonnie leaned back in the chair and allowed the tension to flow out of her limbs. Ethan would be fine, she told herself. She was surprised to feel a small head resting on her knee.

"Brendan?" She stroked the blond hair affectionately. "Are you all right, buddy?"

Brendan lifted a tear-streaked face. "Ethan fell down," he murmured.

"Yes, he did, but he's okay now."

"You sure?"

"I'm positive," she answered, giving the small body a reassuring hug.

Kate handed Bonnie a mug of sugared tea and squatted down beside her. "Drink that," she advised. She pulled Brendan into her lap and cuddled him protectively. They sat quietly while Jennifer handed the remaining children over to their parents.

The center was so unnaturally quiet that Bonnie

closed her eyes for a moment. When she opened them, David was standing above her, smiling tenderly at her. He reached out a hand to help her to her feet. For a moment they were dangerously close, and then he stepped back but kept hold of her hand.

"Ethan's fine. He's sound asleep at my mom's house. Mom says she'll keep him overnight. She told me to take you out for a decent meal."

"Really? Are you sure you feel like doing that?"

"I'm sure. You go on home and get cleaned up, and I'll pick you up in an hour. Is that enough time?"

Bonnie looked down at her stained clothes. "What do you think?" she asked with a rueful smile.

"More than enough," he answered. His voice was suddenly husky. "And, Bonnie, do me a favor? Wear your hair down?" He ran a finger down her cheek. "I'll see you in an hour," he said, tucking her car keys into her trembling fingers.

Chapter Six

"Good heavens, what happened to you? Are you all right?" Liz greeted Bonnie with a mixture of horror and concern in her voice.

"I'm fine. We had a little accident at work. Ethan split his chin; this is his blood, not mine," Bonnie reassured her friend quickly.

"You frightened me. Is Ethan okay?"

"Yes, I think so. David brought him to his mother's house. He's going to spend the night there. His mother told him to take me out to dinner," she added.

"Well, that's a turn in events, isn't it? I suppose you think that's a fine idea."

"You bet I do. I'm going up to change now; he'll be here by seven."

"Then I won't keep you," Liz said gently. "Do you have everything you need?"

"Yes, I think so," Bonnie said gratefully as she sped up the stairs.

By seven o'clock Bonnie was waiting on the porch. She was wearing a black-and-white print dress, and her shining brown hair just touched her shoulders. She had been careful with her makeup and had applied just enough to enhance her fresh complexion and soft brown eyes. When David drove up in a light-blue sedan, she greeted him with an excited smile.

"Where's the truck?" she asked.

"Mom thought her car would be more appropriate," he answered with a grin.

"How nice of her!" Bonnie said as David opened the door for her. His hand on her arm was warm and firm.

Once in the car, he turned to her. "You look wonderful," he told her.

"Thank you," Bonnie said simply. "Actually, you do too," she added, noting David's blue shirt, which complemented his incredible eyes. It was David's turn to turn red as he quickly started the car and pulled out of the driveway.

Once on the road, they both relaxed while David reassured Bonnie that Ethan was fine and sleeping peacefully at his mother's house.

"Where are we going?" she asked as he drove away from Abbotts Hill.

"To a restaurant in Milford that I think you'll like, especially if you like seafood."

"I love it," she replied, settling back contentedly in her seat.

The restaurant was a lovely, rustic inn. Bonnie and David gazed at each other across the candlelit table and realized that they were alone together for the first time. What they would order was so unimportant, although Bonnie's shrimp was delicious and David's baked scrod was perfectly prepared. They toyed with their food, talking all the while, and occasionally their fingers met across the white-linen tablecloth.

They shared a chocolate mousse for dessert, and as Bonnie licked whipped cream from her spoon, David leaned toward her and said quietly, "Bonnie, there's one thing we haven't talked about, and I guess we need to."

Bonnie raised her head slowly. The candlelight glowed on her shining hair and cast becoming shadows across her oval face. She studied his serious expression and didn't speak.

"It's about my marriage—"

"You don't have to tell me about that if you don't want to," she interrupted him.

"I want to," he assured her. "I want everything to be straight between us." He put down his spoon and reached for her hand. The pudding lay forgotten between them.

"I've been divorced for almost three years now, and this is the first time I've cared enough for anyone to even think about. . . . Well, I want you to know what happened between Caroline and me. Caroline and I started going together in high school, and when we graduated, she went to business school and I started college. Even then, we planned to marry when I graduated, but Caroline was impatient. She got a decent job and started saving for the wedding. I would have stuck it out in college, I think, but then my Uncle Jerry had a stroke and the family asked me to take over the printing business. I had worked there every summer since I was fourteen, so I was the logical one.''

"How old were you?" Bonnie asked.

"I was twenty-one at the time and in my junior year. Caroline was delighted. We got married that spring and got our own little place. Everything was okay for a while. Even when we decided to have a baby, I thought we could manage. And we did, we really did, until after Ethan was born. He was such a fussy baby. We were both exhausted, trying to take care of him. Caroline tried very hard. Of course, we never dreamed there was anything really wrong with him. By the time Ethan was diagnosed, Caroline was frightened. She said she needed some time away, and I encouraged her to go. I never dreamed she wouldn't come back.'' David paused and sipped his coffee. He hardly noticed that it had become ice cold.

Bonnie wiped a tear from her eye. "You don't have to say any more," she ventured.

"Yes, I do. Just one more thing. I'm over Caroline,

totally and completely. I don't love her, and I don't hate her. I just feel sorry for her. Do you understand?''

"I think so.''

"Good. Now, would you like an after-dinner drink, or would you like to go for a drive?''

"Let's go for a drive,'' she answered, reaching for her purse.

By the time they returned to the farmhouse, the stars had come out, and they paused on the steps while Bonnie pointed out several constellations to David. She explained that astronomy had been a hobby of her older brother's, and she had spent many a summer's night on the back deck peering through an old telescope. She stood on the top step, counting stars in the Little Dipper, when David on the step below her folded her in his arms and kissed her until the stars shone in her eyes as brightly as they did in the sky.

David called on Saturday morning to tell her that Ethan had spent a restless night, and, as much as he had wished to spend some time with her over the weekend, he thought he had better keep him quietly at home. Bonnie assured him that she understood. After all, they had all the time in the world.

On Monday, Bonnie opened Ethan's journal to find that David had indeed been thinking of her as he had promised. She smiled as she read the following poem:

I wish you
some new love

of lovely things,
and some new forgetfulness
of the teasing things,
and some higher pride
in the praising things,
and some sweeter peace
from the hurrying things,
and some closer fence
from the worrying things.
              John Ruskin

Bonnie was careful with Ethan that week. He seemed fine, if a little pale, but she spent more time with him than usual while Faith managed the rest of the class. Fortunately, he accepted the second trip to the doctor for the removal of the stitches stoically, and the few tears he shed were quickly erased by a trip to Friendly's for an ice-cream cone. David and Bonnie returned to the center in a holiday mood, and, under the curious eye of Jennifer, made quick plans for Friday night.

That Friday was just the first of many companionable times that Bonnie, David, and Ethan spent during the brisk days of fall. September passed swiftly, and Bonnie spared little time for her family in Massachusetts, making excuses for the time spent in Abbots Hill and fending off questions from her concerned parents.

Only to her sister, Maureen, did she disclose her true reason for spending most of her time in New

Hampshire, and Maureen was cautious in her encouragement, reminding her that their parents would be sure to have reservations about her dating a divorced man. Bonnie realized this, but she was sure that when the time came to introduce David to her parents, they would be impressed with him and would approve. But, for now, she was more than content to let the relationship grow slowly and surely from friendship to something more.

By October, Bonnie and Faith had established a close working relationship and were seeing some small successes in the classroom. Ethan had settled down, and there had been no more frightening episodes of out-of-control behavior. Their efforts to teach him to sign were modestly successful, and with David's cooperation Ethan was beginning to communicate more regularly.

Kate was lavish with her praise, and as Halloween approached, there was an air of excitement and well-being at the center that spilled over into Bonnie and David's relationship. Even Liz seemed to have put aside her reservations and often invited David to share a potluck supper on Sunday nights when there were no overnight guests.

One Monday morning in late October, Bonnie found a note in Ethan's journal: *Bonnie, Mom told me to bring you to dinner on Sunday. She says it's time you met the family. I agree.*

Bonnie shivered with excitement. The week seemed

to drag by, although Ethan was unusually mellow and rather consistent in his signing.

On Thursday, Bonnie's step was buoyant as she climbed the steps to the center. She was surprised to find Faith holding Ethan's journal and regarding Bonnie with an odd expression on her face. "Bonnie, Kate wants to talk to you," she said.

"Oh, okay," she replied, wondering why Faith seemed so upset. She tapped on Kate's door and then popped inside.

"Did you want to see me?"

"Yes, please sit down. I have something to tell you."

Bonnie perched in the orange chair and regarded Kate curiously. "Something wrong?" she asked.

"Bonnie, Caroline has come back to town. She called David last night to say that she's staying with her sister and that she wants to see Ethan. She says she misses him and she wants to try to get to know him again."

"Is David going to allow it?"

"He asked my advice, Bonnie, and I told him that he can't keep her from her son. She has a right to see him."

"But he has full custody," Bonnie protested.

"I'm not talking about legal rights, Bonnie. She has a moral right to see him, and Ethan deserves a chance to know his mother."

"Even though she deserted him?"

"That's not like you, Bonnie. I know you have a lot of feeling for Ethan . . . and his father, but if you think about it. . . ."

"Of course, you're right," Bonnie admitted wearily, "but I don't have to like it."

"No, indeed you don't, but I'm going to count on you to help this go smoothly. I told David that Caroline could have her first meeting with Ethan here and that we would try to prepare him for it."

"When is this supposed to take place?"

"On Friday, after the center closes, and, Bonnie, I told David you wouldn't be here for the meeting."

"Why shouldn't I be here?' "

"David and I agreed that Ethan is so attached to you that it would make it more difficult for Caroline to approach him."

Bonnie nodded reluctantly. "How do you suggest I prepare him for seeing his mother again? I don't think he remembers her."

"We can't be sure of that. I don't know what to tell you. Ask Faith for her help; she has good instincts."

"I'll do my best."

"I know you will, and I know what you think is at stake here for you, but please have faith in David. Give him time to work this through."

"I'll try," Bonnie said, leaving the office.

She was surprised to find that she was still clutching Ethan's journal in her hands. Hurriedly she opened it to find a brief message: *Bonnie, I'll call you.*

It was small comfort. She searched out her group of children and hugged each one of them briefly. It was indicative of Ethan's progress that he at least suffered the embrace stoically. Tugging Freddie into her lap, she faced the concerned expression on Faith's pretty face.

"I gather you've heard the news," Bonnie remarked.

Faith nodded. "What can I do to help?"

"I'm supposed to ask you that," Bonnie answered with a wry smile. "Do you have any ideas how to help Ethan accept his mother's return?"

"I think it's my turn to spend the day with Ethan while you work with the other children," Faith replied.

"Would you do that? I would really appreciate it."

"It would be my pleasure. It's time for you to detach yourself, just a little."

"Kate said your instincts were good, and she was right," Bonnie said, hugging her. "And now, kids, let's join the circle," she told the patiently waiting children.

It was a most difficult day for Bonnie. She missed her time with Ethan and was distracted when working with the others. She couldn't resist sitting beside Ethan for lunch or soothing him at naptime, but for most of the day she left him in Faith's hands.

She had to admire Faith's ingenuity when she searched out a book about baby animals and carefully pointed out piglets with the sow, kittens with the cat,

and baby ducks with their mother, all the while croon-
ing to Ethan that everyone has a mother. But judging
by Ethan's customary inattention, it seemed it would
take more than two days to prepare him for such a
momentous change in his life.

Bonnie forced herself to leave a little early so as not
to meet David when he came to pick up Ethan. She
didn't trust herself to confront him face-to-face, and
Kate was quick to agree that it would be far better to
wait for his call.

It was obvious that David didn't share her feelings,
because the phone rang shortly after she arrived at the
farmhouse.

"I thought I would see you," he began abruptly.

"You said you would phone. I thought you
meant—"

"I was wrong. I need to talk to you."

"Maybe it's better this way," Bonnie said miserably.

David sighed his agreement. "Kate told you Caroline is back?"

"Yes, and that she wants to see Ethan. I guess you
have to let her."

"I do. I'll be seeing her tonight to talk things over.
Bonnie, I feel terrible about this, but I'm afraid we'll
have to postpone our dinner with my mom. This just
isn't the right time."

"I understand," Bonnie said softly.

"I don't know what Caroline has in mind, but until I find out, maybe you and I should, well. . . ."

"Stop seeing each other?"

"Just for a little while. I'll keep in touch with you, of course."

"Of course," Bonnie agreed, fighting back tears.

David seemed reluctant to end their conversation, but eventually he realized there was nothing more he could say but a whispered good-bye. Bonnie dropped the phone back into its cradle and sat for a moment in stunned silence.

She didn't hear Liz come into the room until baby Joshua crowed aloud at the sight of her. Bonnie tried to hide her tears, but Liz ignored them, dropped into a wing chair, and regarded her thoughtfully.

"Do you want to talk?" she asked.

"You've heard the news, I gather. No secrets in this town," Bonnie said bitterly.

"Not when you run the general store," Liz agreed lightly.

"There's nothing to talk about," Bonnie said, rising from her chair and moving toward the stairs. Liz reached out a hand and grasped her arm. The baby bounced in her lap and smiled winningly at Bonnie. Bonnie couldn't resist him and took him in her arms to bury her face in his neck.

Liz watched her for a moment in silence, then said, "Give him time, Bonnie. David will work it out."

"That seems to be the consensus of opinion."

"Then it must be right," Liz said cheerfully.

"Then I'll try to believe it," Bonnie answered with a brave smile as she returned the baby to his mother.

Liz followed Bonnie to the stairs and called after her, "I'll expect you at dinner. It's your favorite—turkey pot pie."

"I'll be down," Bonnie promised.

Dinner was a solemn affair, though Liz tried her best to keep the conversation going. But Bonnie was toying with her food, and Tim, a naturally quiet man, seemed unable to break through his natural reserve to comment on the situation, although several times he cleared his throat as a prelude to speech. Finally, over coffee and apple cobbler, he overcame his reticence and spoke. "You know, I went to school with David's sister, Mary Ellen."

Liz looked as surprised as Bonnie at this information.

"I didn't know that," she commented.

"Wasn't important," he said, dipping a spoon into his dessert.

"Is it now?" Liz teased him.

"Only to say, I've known David a long time. He was just a kid when I was in high school, but he used to shoot hoops with us when we hung around the Andersons' house."

"You used to hang around Mary Ellen's house?"

"Liz, that was a long time ago. All I'm saying is, I always thought David was a good guy, especially when he left school to run his uncle's business."

"Well, you could relate to that," Liz said softly.

Tim shot her a look and continued, "He's had a tough time since he married Caroline, but he's always done the right thing, and he'll do it now."

"If that's meant to reassure me, Tim, I'm not sure it does," Bonnie said. "Suppose David thinks the right thing is to get back with Caroline so that Ethan will have his parents together again?"

It was Tim's turn to look surprised. "You wouldn't say that if you knew Caroline," he said shortly.

"Tim's right, Bonnie. That would never work."

But as much as Bonnie would have liked to believe them, she wasn't sure.

Chapter Seven

When Bonnie awoke on Friday morning to a cool, rainy fall day, she wanted to pull the covers over her head and stay in bed. The temptation to call in sick was overwhelming, but soon her responsibility to Ethan and her desire to catch even a glimpse of David forced her to leave her bed and join a sleepy Liz in the kitchen.

"Corn muffin?" Liz offered.

"Love one," Bonnie said cheerfully.

Liz raised an eyebrow quizzically. "New attitude?"

"Positive thinking," Bonnie replied, but when she tried to eat her muffin, it turned to sawdust in her mouth, and she had to content herself with juice and coffee.

Liz removed her dish without comment and dumped the crumbled muffin into a pan she kept to feed the birds. "I guess we'll see you tonight," she said hesitantly.

Bonnie finished her coffee and brought her cup to the sink. "Maybe I'll go home for the weekend."

"Don't do that," Liz cautioned. "David will want to talk to you. Don't run away."

"I'll think about it," Bonnie replied.

When Bonnie left early for school, Liz wisely made no comment. When she arrived in the parking lot, Bonnie sat for a moment in her car. She realized that David might have already dropped Ethan at the center, but it was more likely that he had not yet come. In a moment her hopes were realized when David squeezed the red truck in next to her car. He lifted Ethan from his seat and sat him on the steps of the center while Bonnie left her car and stood waiting for him.

"Good morning," he said quietly.

"Hi," Bonnie answered. "You look tired," she added.

"Didn't sleep very well. How about you?"

"About the same. Is it all set up for tonight?"

"Yes. I understand you won't be here."

"That's right. Kate thought it would be better that way."

"I know. I'm not sure I agree, but she knows best, I guess. Either way, it will be tough on Ethan. I tried to prepare him last night, but it's so hard to know how much he understands. Kate suggested that I show him pictures of Caroline and me with him as a baby, and I did dig some up, but I barely got his attention.''

''We'll keep talking about it today. That's all we can do. I wish you luck.'' Tentatively she reached for his hand and found her fingers locked in his. She had to look away from the pain in his face. ''I have to go,'' she said miserably.

''I know. Can I call you tonight to tell you how it went?''

''Of course. I thought about going home for the weekend, but I decided against it.''

''I'm glad. I'll miss you tonight, but maybe soon everything will be right.''

''Maybe soon,'' Bonnie agreed, taking Ethan by the hand and leading him into the center.

For the second time Bonnie left Ethan in Faith's care for most of the day. At one point she was almost afraid to hope, but it seemed that Ethan missed her and was following her with his eyes. It would be such a break-through if it were true. This day passed almost too quickly and, all too soon, Kate was reminding Bonnie that it was time for her to leave. Bonnie dropped a kiss on Ethan's soft blond hair and said good-bye to Faith and the remaining children.

Jennifer walked Bonnie to the door. ''I don't see why you have to leave,'' she muttered. Bonnie looked at her in surprise. ''Just because she thinks she can waltz back into his life, just like that,'' she continued.

"Jennifer, she has a right to see her child," Bonnie said mildly.

"I'm not talking about Ethan!" Jennifer exclaimed. "I mean David's life. You and David had a good thing going, and now she shows up!"

"Jen, I'm surprised, I thought you wanted David for yourself."

Jennifer blushed. "Oh, Bonnie, I'm not saying I didn't have the biggest crush on him. I mean, after all, he *is* gorgeous, but he's so old—I mean too old for me—but just right for you. Well, you know what I mean, and you guys look so cute together. Well, it's just not fair, you know?"

They were standing beside Bonnie's car, and she reached out and hugged Jennifer. "I know what you mean," she told her solemnly.

On her way to the farmhouse, Bonnie stopped at the MacCreadys' store to see if Liz was behind the counter. She found Tim stocking shelves with jars of honey.

"Liz is on her way home to feed Binky. She said if you dropped in to tell you that we're all going out for Chinese food tonight and that I was not to take no for an answer, so please don't say no and get me in trouble."

Bonnie looked at Tim doubtfully. That was the longest speech she had ever heard him make. "Oh, Tim, I'm not sure. . . ."

"See now, there you go, trying to get me in trouble."

"Okay, okay, I won't say no." Bonnie had to laugh. "Chinese food it is. May I go home and change, or am I a hostage until she returns?"

"You may go home, change, and wait for me there until Joe turns up to take over the store."

"Yes, sir." Bonnie saluted and left the store.

She drove slowly along the back road to the farmhouse, pausing on a hilltop to admire the foliage that had reached a peak of orange, yellow, and russet hues.

She remembered that she and David had planned a trip to Temple Mountain for Sunday afternoon, to show Ethan the view, and felt a pang of disappointment coupled with anxiety. David hadn't mentioned his meeting with Caroline. She wondered what that meant. Perhaps when he called this evening, if in fact he did call, she could ask him. But what if he never called at all?

She found Liz in the kitchen, seated in the rocking chair, a hungry Joshua at her breast.

"How's the young prince today?"

"Ravenous as usual. He'll be done in a minute. Did you stop at the store?"

"Yes, and Tim gave me your message. I'm to join you for dinner, like it or not."

"Is that how he put it? How charming. But you are coming?"

"Since I have no choice, I accept gracefully."

"Good. Are you all right?"

"I'm fine. David is going to call me tonight to let me know how the meeting went."

"Wouldn't you like to be a fly on the wall when Caroline tries to coax a response out of Ethan?"

Bonnie gave Liz a disapproving glance. "Maybe Ethan will surprise us all," she said.

"Oh, come on, Bonnie, sometimes you're too good to be true. Don't tell me you don't hope the whole thing turns into a fiasco and that Caroline just goes back to where she came from?"

Bonnie considered the question. "I don't know," she answered honestly. "Part of me wants Ethan to have a relationship with his mother . . . but most of me wants David and Ethan for myself!"

"Now that's what I like to hear, a fighting spirit," Liz said, rising from the chair with Joshua under her arm like a football. "Now, let's go eat lobster Cantonese."

Bonnie enjoyed dinner in spite of herself. Liz was wickedly amusing, and even Tim stirred himself to tell her droll stories in his laconic fashion. It wasn't until Tim was unlocking the front door and she could hear the phone ringing that the sinking feeling returned to her stomach.

"You answer it," she told Liz. Liz shrugged as she picked up the phone. "MacCreadys' Farm," she said in her usual firm tones. She listened for a moment and then passed the receiver to Bonnie with a casual, "She's right here."

"Hello," Bonnie said hesitantly as Liz pushed poor Tim down the hallway.

"Bonnie? It's me. Are you okay? I tried to reach you earlier."

"Liz and Tim insisted I go out to dinner with them. We just walked in the door."

"That was good of them. I hated to think of you alone." He paused as if reluctant to proceed. "I wish I could come over there, but Ethan is asleep, and I can't leave him. You'll want to know about the meeting, but I don't know where to begin."

Bonnie slumped into the chair by the phone. "Is Ethan all right? It's early for him to be in bed."

"Well, he's not actually in bed. I'm sure he'll be up again later. He fell asleep in my lap, and I just put him on the couch."

Bonnie's heart fell. She knew that was not a good sign. Ethan's sleeping patterns were erratic at best, but for him to fall asleep before nine o'clock was a signal of a major withdrawal. "I gather it didn't go well," she said.

"It's hard to tell. Caroline was very patient. She's changed, Bonnie, I have to admit it. I felt sorry for her, she was so drawn to Ethan. She kept saying how beautiful he is. Of course he wouldn't let her touch him. He clung to Kate and buried his face in her shoulder."

If I had been there, it would have been my arms he hid in, she thought with a pang.

"What's going to happen now?" she asked.

"Well, Caroline is going to stay in town for a while. Her sister, Laurie, is happy to have her. Their parents moved to Florida last winter, so Laurie has been pretty much alone. I agreed to let Caroline spend some time with Ethan at my house or my mom's until he gets to know her again. I don't know what else I can do. . . ." His voice trailed off, as if he expected her to disagree. Bonnie wished she could protest, but she didn't feel that she had the right.

"Bonnie? Are you still there?"

"I'm here," she said quietly. "David, what about us?"

"I don't know. I wish I could tell you, but I just don't know. Seeing Caroline again is so confusing. I need some time to sort things out. Will you be patient, Bonnie?"

"I'll try," she said softly. "Will you call me?"

"I'll keep in touch, I promise," David said in a husky voice.

When Bonnie said good-bye, she went right upstairs to her room. She opened her top drawer and took out the wooden box in which she kept David's notes and the poems he had enclosed in Ethan's journal. She clutched them in her hands as she felt the tears sting her eyes.

Everyone had counseled her to give David time and he would do the right thing, but what if the right thing for David was to give Caroline another chance? What if he was about to let her back into his life?

Well, she thought, *I'm not going to sit around here moping about it.* She pulled her overnight bag down from the closet shelf and began throwing articles of clothing into it. In the morning she would go home and spend some time with her family.

Bonnie's parents were so pleasantly surprised to see her that it was easy to fall into the old patterns of her growing-up years. The warm ambience of her childhood home enfolded her and eased some of the pain and uncertainty she had suffered the night before. She spent part of the afternoon helping her father rake the remaining leaves from the front lawn.

As she helped her mother prepare dinner in the familiar kitchen, she was tempted to tell her all her fears and doubts but realized that this was not the right time to introduce the subject of David and his son. She had so hoped that the next time she returned home, she would be able to share her happiness with her family. But now it seemed there was nothing to share.

After dinner she called her sister, Maureen, who immediately invited her over to spend the night.

"Barney's out of town again, and I'm here alone with the kids. I'll get them to bed, and we can have a good talk. It's been such a long time since we've spent some time together."

Bonnie was sorely tempted but afraid that her parents would be disappointed if she didn't stay with them.

Her mother's face fell when she told her of Maureen's invitation, but she encouraged her to go.

"Go ahead, spend some time with your sister. Will you leave from her house tomorrow?"

"Yes, I guess I will, since she's closer to New Hampshire. You're not too disappointed?"

"Of course not. We were happy to have you here for the day. Besides, maybe you'll tell her what you are so carefully not telling me."

"Mom," Bonnie said, "I don't know what you mean."

"Sure you do. You've been covering up something all day. Did you think I wouldn't guess when you showed up on the doorstep looking like you lost your last friend?"

Bonnie had to laugh. "Am I that transparent?"

"Only to your mother. Dad commented on how well you were looking."

"God bless him. Mom, I'd like to tell you what's bothering me, but I'm just not ready to talk about it. Please try to understand."

"I understand. Whenever you're ready, I'll be here."

Bonnie hugged her mother warmly. "I know that, Mom. I know I can always count on you and Dad."

When she arrived at her sister's house, she found Maureen in the kitchen of the attractive ranch house.

"Is this new wallpaper?"

"Yes, it is, and let me tell you, hanging wallpaper with your husband is a true test of your marriage."

"How did you and Barney make out? Is he really away on business or buried under the willow tree?"

"Well, it was a near thing, but he really is in Chicago for a sales meeting."

"On the weekend?"

"Cheaper air fares. The company is nothing if not thrifty, and, in all honesty, I miss him sorely, even after eight years of marriage." She poured cocoa into mugs and added mini-marshmallows. "Want some Oreos?"

Bonnie laughed. "Just what I need. How did you guess?"

"Chocolate is my cure for everything. Let's take it into the living room. Just don't tell the kids." She loaded a tray with the mugs, napkins, and the box of Oreos. "Wish I had some M&M's, but I'm fresh out."

"This will do fine. I'm sorry I missed the children. Are they asleep?"

"I hope so. It's been a long day." She placed the tray on the coffee table and curled up on the couch with her long legs tucked under her. "It's hard when Barney's not home. They miss him, especially at bedtime."

Bonnie tucked herself into the other end of the couch and looked around the comfortable living room. "It's nice being here. I'd forgotten how much I like this house."

"Now don't go all sentimental on me. You're just feeling all mushy because things are not going well with the new romance. Am I right?" She pulled an Oreo apart and licked off the filling.

"Can everyone see right through me? Mom accused me of holding out on her, but, fortunately, she didn't press the issue. Since she doesn't know a thing about David, this was not the time to introduce the subject."

"Trouble in paradise?"

"Afraid so." Bonnie sipped her cocoa and dismembered an Oreo.

"Well, start talking. We've got all night."

When Bonnie had finished outlining the events of the past few days, Maureen uncurled her legs and leaned forward with her head in her hands.

"What do you think?" Bonnie asked.

"I think your friends in Abbots Hill are giving you good advice, particularly since they know your David a lot longer than you do."

"I hope you're not going to tell me to be patient. I don't think I could take that coming from you. You don't have a patient bone in your body. Admit it."

"To some degree that may be true, but you don't know the whole story. You were only a kid when I met Barney."

"I remember the first time he came for dinner. I was twelve, and I thought he was so handsome, but old. Was he all of twenty-one?"

"Just about. But that was weeks after I met him. I

had gone on a ski weekend from college. I first saw him on the slopes. I didn't ski very well, but he was patient enough to ski with me for a while. It wasn't until we were having dinner in the lodge that someone told me he was engaged, but that his fiancée had gotten the flu at the last minute and told him to go on ahead without her. I was devastated. I spent the next two days avoiding him but watching him the whole time. On the bus going home, he sat down next to me.''

''And you cut him dead, right?''

''I tried to. I asked him if what I had heard was true. He said he was engaged to a girl he had known all his life.''

''What did you do?''

''I changed my seat, but I never forgot him. A few weeks later I went to a frat party, and he was there alone.''

''And the rest, as they say, is history. Did he break it off because of you?''

''I never asked him. I wanted to believe it was mutual.''

''You're eating cookies in the living room!'' a small voice accused them.

Bonnie looked up to find a little girl in footed pajamas standing in the doorway, hands firmly planted on her hips.

''Oh, no,'' Maureen moaned. ''What are you doing out of bed?'' She went immediately on the offensive.

The child rubbed her eyes. "I heard you talking. You woke me up!"

Bonnie rose and picked up her niece. "I'm sorry, Megan. Suppose I carry you up to your bed and read you a story. Will that help?"

"And could I have a cookie too?"

"Don't push your luck," her mother said.

When Bonnie had settled Megan and returned to the living room, Maureen was waiting for her to finish the conversation, but Bonnie was weary and ready for bed. Tomorrow morning she would return to Abbots Hill prepared for whatever lay in store for her.

Chapter Eight

On Monday morning Bonnie waited on the steps for David and Ethan. She was almost afraid to meet David's eyes for fear she would read some message there that she didn't want to receive. But David's face was unreadable except for the lines of fatigue.

"Ethan's not sleeping well," he said.

I'm not surprised, Bonnie thought, but refrained from saying it.

Bonnie took Ethan's journal from David and smiled reassuringly at the boy. "I'll make sure he takes a long nap," she told his father.

"He needs one, but then, so do I. Liz said you went home, after all."

"Yes, I left on Saturday morning. She told me you called on Saturday night."

"I wanted to talk to you. I couldn't call last night,

because Ethan wouldn't go to sleep at all. He was literally climbing the walls. I wrote some notes for you in his journal.''

''Did something special happen?'' Bonnie asked reluctantly. She really didn't want to hear that they had spent the weekend with Caroline.

''Caroline took Ethan out for about an hour. I'm afraid she gave him too much sugar. You know how that affects him. But we've got that all cleared up, so it won't happen again.''

Bonnie looked closely at the child, who was clinging to her hand. His eyes had dark circles under them, and his lips twitched slightly. ''Yes, I see. Well, as long as she understands.''

''It was my fault,'' David said. ''I should have told her what he could eat. Caroline couldn't be expected to know the special diet we have worked out for Ethan.''

She could have asked, Bonnie thought and then scolded herself. *I'm being so unfair,* she thought.

''Don't worry, David. We'll get him back on track,'' she told him.

''I hope so. She'll be seeing him during the week, but not alone. The other thing is, my mom is making Ethan a costume for the Halloween party on Friday. She'll probably drop it off here during the week. I have to go,'' he said reluctantly.

They were still standing on the steps, and several parents had squeezed by them with their children, eye-

ing them curiously. *Can they tell how miserable I am?*
Bonnie wondered.

"Can I call you tonight?" David asked, turning to
leave.

"I'm not sure," Bonnie answered honestly. She led
Ethan into the building, missing the confused look on
David's face.

There was no personal message in Ethan's journal
that day, nor did Bonnie expect one. Ethan was as
difficult as Bonnie had anticipated, and she and Faith
were distressed to note a regression in his behavior.
When David called that evening, their conversation
was brief and unsatisfactory to them both.

On Wednesday afternoon Bonnie was encouraging
Ethan to swirl blue finger paint when Kate called her
attention to David's mother, who stood watching her
work.

"I can't believe you can get him to do that. Ethan
doesn't like to get messy."

"I know," Bonnie agreed, "it's been a struggle,
but I think he's beginning to enjoy it. You should see
him do it with chocolate pudding!"

"I guess you know I'm Ethan's grandma. We met
at the parade."

"Yes, of course I remember you, Mrs. Anderson."

"Please call me Helen. I've been meaning to stop
in for a long time to tell you what a great job you're
doing with Ethan, but then you were supposed to come
to the house, until everything changed. I want you to

know I don't approve of what's going on. I don't think it's a bit good for Ethan, for one thing.''

Bonnie hesitated. She sensed that this wasn't a conversation she should be having with David's mother, but it was comforting to know that she seemed to be on her side.

''Is that Ethan's costume for the party?'' she asked, indicating the shopping bag in her hand.

Helen Anderson smiled and accepted the change of subject. ''It is indeed. I spent the whole weekend working on it, and he absolutely refuses to wear it. Maybe you'll have better luck with him.'' She pulled a rich green suit from the bag and held it up. ''I thought I'd make him Peter Pan. I knew he wouldn't wear anything over his face, so I just made a suit with feet and this cute little green hat. . . .''

''It's wonderful!'' Bonnie exclaimed. ''He won't put it on?''

''Nope. He stiffens out like a board, and there's no way to stuff him in. I thought I'd bring it along and let you try. Last year I made this great clown suit, but no luck.'' She shrugged and turned to leave. Bonnie walked with her to the door.

''Bonnie, I just want to say one thing. No, now don't try to stop me. I'm worried about my boy. I want David to be happy, and Caroline is not the person to do it. His dad says I should mind my own business, and he's right, so I haven't said a word to David, but

I'm telling you, Caroline can't leave town soon enough to suit me.''

After Helen left, Bonnie returned to the children with a smile on her face. Faith was trying to show the Peter Pan costume to Ethan, but he had his little face turned resolutely aside. ''Helen Anderson seems to be a very nice person,'' Bonnie said.

''And a wise one,'' Faith added.

After a few minutes Faith abandoned her attempt to interest Ethan in his costume and perched the little green hat on her own head. The other little boys giggled, but Ethan was unimpressed. ''What are you going to be for Halloween, Miss Bonnie?'' Tina asked.

''That's right,'' Bonnie said, ''I need to decide, don't I? What do you suggest?''

''I think you should be a princess,'' Pammy declared.

''I think a princess is beyond my abilities, honey.''

''Do you sew?'' Faith asked.

''Me? You're kidding. Not even hems and buttons.''

''Maybe I can help you. I could alter my costume from last year to fit you,'' she offered.

''I'd appreciate that. What did you wear last year?'' she asked curiously.

Faith smiled and shook her head. ''Let me surprise you. I'll bring it in tomorrow for you to try on.''

''All right,'' Bonnie agreed. ''I don't suppose you're going to tell me what you're wearing this year.''

"You're right, I'm not," Faith agreed, rising from the mat to put away the paints.

On Thursday morning Bonnie found a short note clipped to the journal. It read:

Bonnie,
We need to talk. Will you meet me for coffee after work
tonight? Caroline's sister, Laurie, will be picking up
Ethan. Please.

Love,
David

Bonnie held the note in her hand for a few moments before slipping it into her pocket. As much as she yearned to see David alone, she was weary of the conversations that just went in circles, resolving nothing. If she did agree to see him, she was determined that this time some sort of decision would be reached.

She found her group of children clustered around Faith, who held a large paper bag. Both of the little girls looked about to burst with excitement.

"Oh, Miss Bonnie, wait until you see," Pammy said, her elfin face wreathed in smiles.

"I think someone's been peeking," Bonnie teased.

"Oh, no, Miss Faith showed us the whole thing."

"Well, then, Miss Faith, show me too."

Faith emptied the bag onto a mat. There lay a gingham dress, white apron, striped stockings, and red-yarn wig. The perfect Raggedy Ann costume. "I hope you have flat shoes," she said.

"This is beautiful!" Bonnie exclaimed. "Are you sure you don't want to wear it again?"

"Oh, no, this is for you. I think I'll just have to take some tucks in the waistline. I can do it during naptime."

Bonnie held the dress up in front of her and twirled in a circle to the delight of the children. Even Ethan's attention was caught by the motion, and he rose to twirl with her. "Oh, dear," Bonnie said and stopped in her tracks, but it was too late. Ethan continued his spinning in wider and wider circles that took him far into the room.

"He hasn't done that in a long time," Faith whispered.

"My fault," Bonnie replied. "I got him started."

"No, not at all. He's been slowly regressing, Bonnie. I haven't wanted to admit it, but I'm sure you've seen it too. He doesn't sign anymore, and his nails are bitten to the quick," Faith said sadly.

"I know," Bonnie admitted. "I was planning to talk to Kate today."

"I think you should. I'm a little worried about tomorrow. The Halloween party may be too much for him. Maybe it would be better if someone could keep him at home. I'm sure Mrs. Anderson would do it if we asked."

"You're probably right. The poor lady, she spent

all that time making his costume, and we can't even get him to wear it.''

"She understands. Talk to Kate, see if she agrees.''

Bonnie spent ten minutes with Kate in her untidy office. Kate was sympathetic and promised to observe Ethan during the day. "If he's that close to the edge, then of course you're right. All the children and staff dressed in costume might thoroughly disorient him. I've been reading his journal, and I understand that his sleep is disturbed again. Is he spinning or climbing?''

"He was spinning this morning, and we're having trouble keeping his shoes and socks on his feet.''

"Okay. I'll check on him during the day, and I'll talk to David when he comes to pick him up tonight.''

Bonnie hesitated. "David isn't taking Ethan home tonight. He wants me to meet him for coffee. He said Caroline's sister, Laurie, will be picking up Ethan.''

Kate scowled. "I don't like the sound of that. I'll call him at work.''

Bonnie returned to Faith and the children to find that Ethan had exhausted himself and was curled on the mat in a fetal position. "Kate is going to observe,'' she told Faith quietly.

Ethan's behavior continued to be erratic for the rest of the day. One minute he was in frantic motion and the next slumped in lethargy. Kate was unobtrusive, but Bonnie was aware of her presence. While the children were outside, she took Bonnie aside. "I spoke to David. I told him about my reservations, but he said he couldn't get in touch with Laurie. She'll be here early for Ethan. I can't refuse to let him go; she has David's permission. I did tell him that we need to have a conference with him and Caroline early next week.''

''What about tomorrow?''

''We'll let Ethan come, but we'll watch him closely. At the first sign of trouble, I'll take him to Helen Anderson. I've already spoken to her. She's just as worried as we are.''

Bonnie was relieved and glad to benefit from Kate's expertise. Kate patted her arm and started to walk away, but turned back for a moment. ''Oh, and, Bonnie, when we have that conference next week, I'll need you here. I'll let you know which day.''

Bonnie was singing quietly to Ethan when Kate appeared at her side, accompanied by a slim, dark-haired woman.

''Bonnie, this is Laurie Miller, Ethan's aunt. Laurie, this is Bonnie Delaney, Ethan's teacher.''

Bonnie rose to shake the young woman's hand. She was surprised by the hostility in Laurie Miller's face. She barely extended her fingertips and withdrew them immediately. ''I've come for Ethan,'' she stated boldly.

''Yes, I know,'' Bonnie answered coolly. ''I'll have him ready in a minute. I just have to get his jacket.''

''I'm in a hurry,'' the woman said. ''I have to meet his mother at McDonald's.''

Ethan watched her with no sign of recognition in his

hooded eyes. He stood stiffly as Bonnie slipped his arms into the sleeves of his baseball jacket, but when his aunt tried to take his hand, he pressed against Bonnie's legs.

"Don't give me a hard time, Ethan," Laurie Miller said in an exasperated voice.

"You'd better walk out with him, Bonnie," Kate said blandly, watching Laurie's face. She shot Bonnie a venomous glance but didn't say a word.

Bonnie led Ethan quietly out of the building and walked him to the waiting car. She strapped him into the front seat and then turned to find Laurie regarding her curiously.

"I think he'll be all right now," Bonnie said.

"Oh, he'll be fine, just as soon as he sees his mom. He's just crazy about her, you know." She narrowed her eyes, and her lips twisted in a smile. "Now that his folks are back together again, you'll see a big change in him." She slammed the car door and started to walk around to the driver's side. "Maybe he won't even go to school here anymore," she called. "My sister doesn't like this place much." The gravel spun under her wheels as she drove away.

Bonnie had agreed to meet David shortly after five at the local diner for coffee. She couldn't get Laurie Miller's parting shot out of her mind. She almost told Faith what Laurie had said, but she couldn't bear to repeat it. When she arrived at the Mountain Diner, she found David seated in a red-leather booth, watching the front door anxiously. When she had seated herself across from him, he reached out and took both of her hands in his. His grip was so tight as to be almost painful.

"I'm so glad to see you," he said as the waitress plopped mugs of coffee in front of them.

Bonnie was afraid to speak for fear she would reveal her feelings. There was too much to be settled first. She pulled her hands away and gripped her mug tightly.

"Kate tells me you're concerned about Ethan," David began.

"Aren't you?"

"Of course I am," he said wearily. "Caroline is trying very hard with him, but he's so distant. I guess she needs more time. Actually, he's at his best when the three of us are together," he said miserably.

"I see."

"Do you really? This may be important for Ethan. Maybe having his mother back will make him feel more secure. I owe him that chance, Bonnie."

"Of course you do," she agreed, "but so far Ethan seems to be losing ground." She carefully told him about Ethan's disturbing behavior that day.

"And you think this is because of Caroline's return?"

"I don't know," Bonnie admitted.

"Kate told me she's setting up a meeting. Will you be there?"

"Yes, I will. It should be early next week, if Caroline agrees."

"I'm sure she will. It's important to her too. You know, Bonnie, I really appreciate your concern for Ethan, especially since things are so confused between us."

Bonnie was chilled by the formality of his words. *Confused* was not the word she would have chosen for the state of their relationship. The parting words of Laurie Miller were ringing in her ears: "*Now that Ethan's parents are back together again. . . .*" Then she thought of David's statement: "*Ethan's at his best when the three of us are together.*"

"Well, of course, I'm concerned for Ethan. He is my student." She matched David's formal tones. "Thanks for the coffee, David, but I really must be going." She stood up and squared her shoulders. "Oh, and, David," she added with a smile, "if you have any problems with Ethan over the weekend, I suggest you give Kate a call. I have a lot of plans and may not be home." She managed to maintain the smile until she was safely in her car, where she could let her tears fall.

When she reached the farmhouse, she found Liz in the kitchen, stirring a pot of beef soup. The baby was sitting in his infant seat in the middle of a hooked rug. Bonnie squatted down in front of him. "Hi, Binky. How's my boy?"

"Joshua is a crabby boy today, thank you, and, by

the way, we've decided to stop calling him Binky. Tim is afraid the name will follow him into adulthood and he'll hate us forever.''

"Seems unlikely, but I'll try to oblige since I'm still trying to live down my own childish nickname of Bunny.''

"Bunny, eh? I kind of like that," Liz said.

"Oh, please, don't make me sorry I mentioned it.''

"Don't worry, I'll just tuck it away for blackmail purposes someday. How was your day? Ethan still acting up?''

"It was not a good day," Bonnie began and went on to tell Liz everything that had happened, including her conversation with David.

Liz looked thoughtful for a moment. "You were pretty hard on David, weren't you?''

"Oh, Liz, what would you have done? After what Caroline's sister said and then David talking to me as if I had just a passing interest in Ethan!''

"Whoa, slow down there. First of all, you can't believe a word Laurie Miller says. That whole family has a history of taking liberties with the truth, to put it politely. As for poor David, I guess by now he doesn't know which end is up. He only wants what's best for Ethan. We just have to figure out how to make him see that the best thing for both of them is you.''

Bonnie had to smile. "And how do we do that, oh, wise one?''

"I told you, that's what we have to figure out. First

we eat this wonderful soup of mine, and then we make a plan.''

''Aren't we going to wait for Tim?''

''Not tonight. He had to stop at his mom's to talk to Joe, so we're on our own, just us and Joshua.''

''I don't think he's going to add much to the plan.''

''You never know,'' Liz said with a grin.

Chapter Nine

The next morning Bonnie felt her spirits lift as she donned the Raggedy Ann costume that Faith had altered so carefully for her. She pulled her hair into a tight knot on the top of her head and fitted the red wig over it. Then she carefully applied her makeup with bright circles of rouge on her cheeks. She had to smile at her reflection in the mirror.

She rushed through her breakfast, trying not to smudge her makeup, while Tim had difficulty keeping a straight face each time he looked up from his cereal. Finally, as she was slipping into her jacket, he leaned back in his chair and drawled, ''Is that a new look for you, Bonnie? I kinda like it.''

Feeling considerably more cheerful, Bonnie drove to the center. She hoped to be safely inside before David arrived, assuming that he wouldn't seek her out.

She wanted to enjoy the Halloween party and postpone all thoughts of their relationship until the weekend. She was met at the door by Kate, dressed in a jester's outfit, complete with bells on her toes.

"How cute! Did you make your costume?" Bonnie asked.

"Afraid not." Kate twirled around, bells ajingle. "This is more of Faith's handiwork. I love it so much, I wear it every year."

"What is Faith wearing today?" Bonnie asked.

"Wait until you see her." Kate couldn't contain a giggle. "She's in the other room with Ethan. David dropped him off early for some reason."

To avoid seeing me, Bonnie thought. "How is Ethan?" she asked.

"So far, so good. I'll be watching him, though. Go on in. Faith managed to put his hat on him somehow, and the other children are dying to show off their costumes."

Bonnie walked across the wide pine boards past an assortment of pirates, princesses, and ninja turtles, pausing to admire a costume or straighten a mask. The children were already in a state of excitement at nine o'clock in the morning.

She was almost across the room when she felt a small body attach itself to her legs. "Miss Bonnie, look at me!"

She looked down into a green goblin mask. "Oh,

my goodness,'' she exclaimed, ''I don't know who it is.''

''It's me! It's me!'' a familiar voice piped up.

''Well, it could be Brendan, but, no, I guess not,'' she said doubtfully. Chubby hands whipped the mask from a blond head.

''It *is* Brendan!'' Bonnie exclaimed, hugging the small boy to her side. ''Come with me,'' she invited.

In the next room she found her class in their usual spot but transformed by their costumes. Both of the little girls were dressed as princesses, complete with crowns and wands, one in pink and the other in blue. Freddie's sweet face was wreathed in smiles as he struggled to his feet to display his Batman outfit. Joel giggled and fingered his Dracula sideburns self-consciously.

But it was Faith whom they were anxious for her to see, because Faith was a pumpkin! Seated cross-legged on the mat with Ethan close beside her, she could make anyone smile. Her legs were encased in green tights while her body was enclosed in a wire frame covered with orange fabric and stuffed to pumpkin shape. On her blond head was a felt cap closely resembling a stem.

Bonnie clapped her hands. ''Can you stand up?'' she asked.

''Of course,'' Faith replied, levering herself to her feet with some difficulty. She plumped her costume into place. ''Do you like it?'' she asked.

"It's wonderful!"

"You can wear it next year if it survives the day," she said ruefully. "I don't think it's too practical." She moved slowly away from Ethan, who seemed fascinated by the texture of the orange fabric. He followed her closely, totally ignoring Bonnie, whom he did not seem to recognize.

"Well, you've certainly made a hit with Ethan," Bonnie observed.

"Yes, something about the color or perhaps the shape appeals to him," she agreed. "I can't seem to detach him."

"At least we'll know where he is," Bonnie commented, gathering up the children for the morning circle.

The circle was particularly successful that morning since most of the children were more than willing to stand in the center to display their costumes. Even shy Pammy was coaxed to show off her princess outfit. It was no surprise to the teachers to have Brendan anxious to take center stage in his goblin suit, but his announcement to one and all did cause Kate to raise an eyebrow.

"Guess what?" he piped up. "My daddy is coming to see me soon!"

Everyone clapped as he bowed and relinquished the center to another child. Meanwhile Kate had moved around the room to where Martha stood and pulled her aside for a whispered consultation. "What's up?" Bonnie asked Faith.

"There's a restraining order against Brendan's father. Let's hope this is just Brendan's overactive imagination speaking," she replied.

When circle time was over, Bonnie and Faith took their group—and Brendan, who was determined to spend the day with them—into the smaller room to read Halloween books and play simple games. Ethan seemed to handle the change in schedule calmly and, except for his excessive attachment to Faith's costume, weathered the morning very well.

By the time the children had finished their lunch, Faith was feeling rumpled and weary from Ethan's constant clinging, so Bonnie suggested that once she had settled Ethan down for his nap, she remove the pumpkin and put her feet up for a few minutes. Faith was grateful for the break and was quietly doing paperwork in Kate's office when Ethan began whimpering in his sleep.

Bonnie hurried to his side and knelt beside him on the mat. He was thrashing wildly with his eyes closed. She leaned over him, murmuring in a soothing manner. Suddenly his eyes flew open and focused on her face. In disbelief he saw the orange hair and the red-circled cheeks. He screwed up his face in dismay and screamed.

Within moments, Kate was at his side, gathering him up in her arms. She quickly discarded her jester cap so he was able to twist his fingers in her familiar dark curls and bury his tear-streaked face in her neck. "It's okay, Ethan," she told him calmly. "Look at me, baby. It's Kate."

Watching them rocking together, Bonnie remembered with a pang that Ethan had been Kate's child long before he was hers.

"I'm sorry," Bonnie said softly. "I never thought. . . ."

"Not your fault. We were on borrowed time with him, anyway. I'll call his grandma as soon as he's calmed down."

Kate stood up slowly with Ethan clutched to her slim frame, his legs wrapped around her middle. She grinned ruefully at Bonnie. "I guess I'll just take him along to the office," she added. She narrowed her eyes and whispered over the child's head, "I just can't wait to meet with his mother!"

Bonnie walked along with them, being careful to stay out of Ethan's line of vision.

"Have you set a date for the meeting yet?" she asked.

"Not yet, but I'm hoping for Tuesday evening after the center closes. I'll let you know as soon as I confirm it with Caroline."

When they reached the office, Kate slipped inside and deposited Ethan into Faith's lap. Faith had removed the pumpkin shape and was sitting in the orange chair in her green tights and turtleneck sweater. Ethan perched on her knee and worried a thumbnail with his teeth, his gaze fixed on the orange pumpkin in the corner.

"Ethan's going home?"

"As soon as possible," Kate replied, lifting the phone.

Once Ethan was safely in Helen Anderson's care, Bonnie and Faith returned to their class and tried to make Halloween pleasant for the remaining children. Faith had slipped back into her pumpkin and was helping Joel draw a witch on a broom when she heard an irritated voice.

"Where's Ethan?" She turned to find Laurie Miller confronting her. "I met that kid Jennifer on the steps, and she said he would be in here with you."

Faith regarded her calmly. "Ethan went home with his grandmother. He was a little upset. Perhaps you would like to speak to his teacher." She looked around for Bonnie, who had taken Pammy to the bathroom.

"I don't need to see her. Ethan's mother wanted to see him in his costume. She's waiting outside in my car."

Faith decided not to tell her that Ethan wasn't wearing his costume. "Perhaps if you call Mrs. Anderson . . ." she suggested, steering her toward the door. Faith saw Bonnie emerge from the bathroom and indicated that she stay away.

"I'm not about to call that woman. Caroline can

handle this herself,'' she declared, grasping the door-knob of the heavy oak door.

Faith stepped aside to allow her to pass through the door, but Laurie pulled it open with a vengeance and swung it wide, effectively squashing Faith and her pumpkin against the wall.

''Oh, sorry,'' she said, slamming the door behind her.

Faith looked down at the wreckage of chicken wire that surrounded her body and then slowly made her way back to the classroom.

''Bonnie,'' she said, ''I don't think you'll want to wear this costume next year.''

Bonnie had a miserable weekend. David didn't call, but she hardly expected him to, since she had been so cool to him at their last meeting. Liz tried to keep her busy and even solicited her help in the kitchen since she had a houseful of guests. Bonnie had become quite adept at muffins and waffles, and since Tim always made himself unavailable on such occasions, Liz was grateful for her help.

By the time the folks had left on Sunday night, Bonnie and Liz were exhausted. Tim, feeling a little guilty, offered to put Joshua to bed, while the women sat with their feet up in the family room.

''Thanks for the help,'' Liz told Bonnie wearily. ''I couldn't manage without you. Now that Joshua is demanding more of my time, I think I'll have to stop offering Sunday-night supper. I can't rely on you being here every weekend; it's not fair.''

''That's all right; I didn't have anything else to do.''

''Feeling a little sorry for ourselves, are we?''

''More than a little sorry,'' Bonnie admitted.

''May I point out that you told David not to call?''

''Leave Bonnie alone, Liz. She's a big girl; she can handle her own life,'' Tim said from the doorway. He was holding a huge bowl of popcorn. ''I have a surprise for you gals that will cheer you both up.''

''Popcorn is no surprise; we could smell it popping,'' Liz said.

''Not the popcorn—this!'' He flipped a videotape into her lap.

''*Casablanca!* You're a wonder! Just what we needed.'' She rose to insert the tape into the machine. ''We're all set now, Bonnie. We can both have a good cry.''

Monday dawned cool and gray. Bonnie stood by her window and examined the leafless trees and withered grass. *November,* she thought. *Pilgrims and turkeys.* She dressed in old jeans and a worn sweatshirt. A good day to clean off those bookshelves and rearrange the toys. She pulled her hair into a ponytail and scrubbed her face clean of makeup.

Bonnie arrived at the center early and was busy pulling books from the shelves when Kate came to tell her that Ethan wouldn't be in school that day.

"David said he had a bad weekend. He didn't elaborate, but I gather Ethan's still not sleeping. My guess would be too much sugar again," she added. "By the way, I've set up the meeting with Caroline and David for tomorrow night. I hope we get some answers. I'm worried about that child." She started to walk away and then returned. "Oh, Bonnie, I know Brendan spends a lot of time with you. If he should mention his father again, I'd appreciate it if you would tell me."

Bonnie agreed, and Kate left her to her busywork. She accomplished a lot that day. Without Ethan to occupy a considerable amount of her time, she was able to give the other boys some individual attention. She rearranged the toys and organized the bookshelves. Even with the children helping and hindering the progress, she was satisfied with the results.

By late afternoon she was feeling tired and grubby, so she left Freddie, the only one of their group left in the center, in Faith's care and headed for the bathroom to clean up a bit. As she was passing Kate's office, she heard her call out.

"Bonnie? I was just coming to find you. We've had a change in plans. The meeting with Caroline and David will be tonight instead of tomorrow. Hope that's okay with you."

Bonnie looked down at her spotted sweatshirt and dirty jeans in dismay.

"Would you like to go home and change your clothes?" Kate asked sympathetically.

"No, that's all right," she answered and continued on to the bathroom, where she washed her hands and face and retied her ponytail. She examined her reflection in the mirror and shrugged.

After all the children and staff had left for the day, Kate led Bonnie to the foyer, where she reached high above her head and unbolted the door to the attic. She picked up a heavy-duty flashlight from the bottom step and switched it on. She and Bonnie climbed the narrow steps to a large, dusty room, where Kate pulled a chain attached to a lone light bulb in an ancient fixture.

"I didn't realize there was so much room up here."

Kate handed Bonnie two wooden chairs. "So far we only use it for storage, but someday I hope to move my office up here. It needs a lot of work, but it would be nice to have room to stretch now and then."

They carried the chairs down the stairs, where Kate replaced the flashlight on the bottom step and bolted the door. "Needless to say, we don't allow the children up there. There's a bolt on the other side, too, in case I need to do some rearranging. The staff has a tendency to pile a lot of stuff up there, and it clearly becomes a fire hazard."

They set the chairs in a semicircle in the smaller classroom. Kate dragged her desk chair from her office and added it to the others. Even with the overhead lights switched on, the room seemed desolate without the children.

"Five chairs? Is someone else coming?"

"I invited Helen Anderson. As a caretaker, she might have something to contribute," Kate replied. "She also knows Caroline quite well and might have some insight into what is going on."

"For a moment I was afraid you had included Caroline's sister, Laurie."

Kate grinned. "No, I doubt that would be very constructive." She moved to the window. "I think I hear David's truck. By the way, Bonnie, don't let Caroline surprise you. She's nothing like her sister, Laurie. They're as different as chalk and cheese, at least on the surface."

Despite Kate's warning, Bonnie was startled by the sight of David standing in the doorway with his ex-wife by his side. Bonnie had expected to see a younger version of Laurie Miller's hard good looks. She was unprepared for Caroline's fragile beauty. Caroline was a small woman with a gently curved figure, dressed in a light cashmere sweater, with matching slacks in a becoming shade of teal. Her dark-blond hair was pulled back into an expertly executed French braid, and her pale, manicured hand rested gently on David's arm.

Bonnie thrust her hands behind her back and wondered how she could avoid shaking hands. But if Kate noticed her discomfort, she chose to ignore it and proceeded to extol her virtues as Ethan's teacher.

"I'm so glad to meet you. I've heard a lot about you," Caroline said in her soft voice, extending her slender hand. A waft of perfume reached Bonnie as she grasped the soft hand in her strong fingers.

It was only after he had seated Caroline that David met Bonnie's eyes. His expression was a mixture of concern and pain. But it was so good to see him. Bonnie wanted to reach out and touch him, and he seemed to read this in her eyes because he handed her Ethan's journal in such a way as to brush his fingers against her wrist.

"How is Ethan? We missed him today."

"He's much better. He had a tough weekend. I wrote it all in his journal."

"I'm afraid that was my fault," Caroline said with a disarming smile. "David told me about too much sugar, but they had the cutest cookies at the bakery, little gingerbread men that looked like scarecrows, you know? Ethan really liked them, and I let him eat two."

When Bonnie didn't comment, Caroline went on, "It won't happen again, I promise." She leaned forward anxiously in her seat. David sat down beside her and patted her arm wordlessly.

Bonnie sat in the chair on the end of the row and started to open the journal.

"Where is Ethan now?" she asked.

"My dad offered to take him for a ride in his car so Mom could come to the meeting," David said. "She should be here any minute."

Before Bonnie could wonder where Kate was hiding

herself, she came into the room with Helen Anderson by her side.

"Sorry I'm late," Helen said breathlessly. "Dad and I had a terrible time getting Ethan into his clothes." She sat at the other end of the row opposite Bonnie and smiled in her direction. Kate took the remaining seat on Caroline's right and consulted her clipboard.

"Okay, then, we can get started. I know we all share the same concern for Ethan. Bonnie, why don't you begin?"

Bonnie pulled her notes from the pocket of her jeans. By directing her attention to Helen and David, she gradually gained confidence and made a concise report. When she had finished, Kate questioned David and his mother. It became obvious that the behavior that distressed them at the center was being repeated at home. The restless, erratic wandering, the spinning and nail-biting combined with the latest habit of removing his clothes seemed even more pronounced in his home environment.

Helen seemed close to tears. "Dad and I can't take him out anymore, not even to McDonald's, which was his favorite."

Kate made some notes and finally turned her attention to Ethan's mother.

"Caroline, I know you have only been back with Ethan for a short time, but perhaps you have something you would like to tell us about his behavior with you."

Caroline hesitated and looked to David for reassurance. ''Well, I don't know. He's such a beautiful little boy, but he's so hard to get close to. He hardly ever lets me touch him, and of course he doesn't talk at all. But I'm trying, you know, I really am. And I'm determined to be his mother again, no matter how long it takes.''

''Well, that's it then,'' Kate announced while Bonnie reluctantly met David's glance, which reflected sadness and resignation.

Chapter Ten

"Well, that was interesting," Kate said after the others had left. Bonnie slumped in her chair and did not answer, so Kate sat beside her and nudged her with her knee. "Any wonderful insights to share?"

Bonnie tucked her hair into her ponytail holder and examined her fingernails. "I need a manicure," she answered.

Kate laughed. "Caroline has that effect on me too. But, in addition to a desire for a complete make-over, what can we take away from today's meeting?"

"I'm not sure. Is it too simplistic to assume that Ethan is reacting badly to his mother's return, or am I too biased to have a valid opinion?"

"No, to both questions. Ethan was progressing nicely this fall. I was impressed with the progress he was making in sign language. It can't be just a coincidence. We have to connect his regression to Caroline's return. The question is, why is this happening? She sounds reasonable enough when she talks about how hard she's trying and how patient she is. Except for stuffing him with sugar, there's nothing I can put my finger on, unless it's simply the change in his routine.''

''That doesn't seem to be enough. I changed his routine, and it only took a short while for him to settle down. There's something else. . . .''

''Well, I guess we'll have to wait and see. I have to go home before poor Mark sends out the troops. Read over your notes—maybe something will strike you—and I'll do the same. Perhaps it will be just a matter of time, but somehow I doubt it.''

Kate and Bonnie walked to the door, and Kate locked up the center. Noticing the expression on Bonnie's face, she placed a slender arm around her shoulders. ''Don't take Caroline too seriously. Even if she does manage to reassume her role as Ethan's mother, that doesn't make her David's wife.''

Bonnie understood what Kate was trying to tell her, and she only wished she could believe it was true.

The next day Bonnie told Faith about the meeting. She seemed disappointed. ''Then nothing was decided?'' she asked.

''Afraid not. What did you hope for?''

''I'm not sure. A simple solution, I suppose.''

"No such luck. I guess we just continue to monitor him and give Caroline more time to establish herself."

"Sounds foolish to me," Faith said simply and walked away.

Ethan was reasonably calm that day and, except for the dark circles under his eyes that denoted a lack of sleep, seemed to have recuperated from his troublesome weekend. He seemed content to be back in the classroom, and, while he ignored any attempts to encourage him to sign for his wants or needs, he didn't indulge in any disturbing behavior.

Kate surprised Bonnie by spending some time with the group, but even this departure from routine didn't seem to upset Ethan. She brought Brendan with her, and he swirled finger paint happily with Joel and Freddie. Kate watched him for a moment and then asked him about two blobs in the middle of his picture.

"That's my daddy and me. He'll be here soon," Brendan told her cheerfully.

"How do you know that?" Kate asked him.

"He told me so." He pulled Kate down to whisper in her ear. "He called me at the baby-sitter. Don't tell."

Kate frowned, but she calmly admired the boy's pictures and then excused herself, saying she had to make some phone calls.

When she returned, Kate had a distracted look. She took Bonnie aside for a whispered conference.

"I just called Brendan's mother, Donna Morgan, at

her job. She doesn't know a thing about any phone calls, but the sitter she uses is some distant relative of her husband's, so anything is possible. I also called the police chief, Andy Boudreau. He said Gary Morgan was released from jail in Massachusetts last week and could be heading this way."

"What do we do now?"

"I'm not sure. Andy suggested I talk to Brendan and see what I can find out. I have Donna's permission to move Brendan if necessary, but Andy would rather we didn't take him from the center."

Kate approached the table where the child was happily making snakes from Play-Doh. "Hi, Bren, want some juice?"

"Snack time?"

"Not yet, but I'm thirsty, aren't you?"

"Sure," he replied, sliding from his chair. He put his hand confidently in Kate's and walked with her to the kitchen.

"Is there a problem?" Faith asked Bonnie.

"Brendan's father may be back in town. Kate called his mother and the police."

"That's not good," Faith said with a worried frown. "There was a lot of trouble before he was arrested for passing bad checks. He tried to take Brendan from the sitter's. That's when Kate took him here. Mr. Morgan is not allowed on the grounds."

Bonnie and Faith returned to their own children and were busy until lunchtime. When they brought the group to the table at noon, they found that Brendan was back with Martha, his usual teacher, and Kate was closeted in her little office with Chief Boudreau.

Martha pulled Bonnie aside. "Gary Morgan has been seen in town. He's looking for Brendan."

"Perhaps he just wants to see him," Bonnie said.

"No, Brendan says his dad told him he's going to take him on a trip to Disney World. He can't wait to see him."

"What's going to happen?"

"I don't know. The chief is still in with Kate. I offered to take Brendan home with me, but he said no, it will be easier to protect him here."

Just then Kate emerged from her office, followed by a burly policeman. Little Emily, ponytail bobbing, ran to his side and clutched his legs. He scooped her into his arms and hugged her enthusiastically.

Martha smiled. "He's Emily's dad. We have no trouble with police coverage here."

After Bonnie had been duly introduced to Chief Boudreau, the chief sent his daughter back to Greta and informed the women that Gary Morgan was indeed in town and reported to be armed with a rifle.

"Clearly violating his parole. Have to pick him up," he stated.

"Has he approached Donna?" Martha asked.

"Not yet, but he went to the sitter's and scared the heart out of her. She's his second cousin, but when she saw that gun, she slammed her door and locked it.

Then she called me. She says she told him Brendan wasn't there; that he was at day care. There are only two other centers in town, so it won't take him long to zero in on this one.''

''Are you sure you don't want me to take Brendan to my house?'' Martha asked.

''Nope, too dangerous. We'll keep him here.''

''What about the other children?'' Bonnie asked.

''I can answer that,'' Kate said. ''We can't empty the center. We'd need permission from every parent to move the children. I'm calling the ones I know can come for their children, but most of them will have to stay.''

''Don't worry, ladies, we plan to be very visible. There will be squad cars parked across your driveway and men posted all across the back. If he so much as drives down 101, we'll have him. There are only two entrances to this place, right?''

''There are the bulkhead doors to the basement, but they bolt from the inside,'' Kate replied.

''Where are the cellar stairs? I'll take care of that right now,'' Boudreau said.

When he emerged from the basement, he nodded his head in satisfaction. ''All secure, ladies,'' he announced.

Bonnie tried to feel reassured but couldn't control a shiver of fear. When Boudreau had left, Kate returned to her office and continued calling those parents who she knew could retrieve their children. As the day

progressed, many anxious parents climbed the center
steps after being questioned by the officers in the patrol
cars parked all around the building.

A phone call to the regional high school advised
Jennifer and the other teenagers not to report for work
that day. As the population in the center decreased,
Martha, Greta, and Faith reluctantly left for the day.

By late afternoon all of Bonnie's children had been
picked up except Freddie, whose parents worked in a
local factory. He and Brendan were quietly working
with Lego blocks. Bonnie and Kate stayed close beside
them, but the late-afternoon light was fading, and they
were trying to decide if it would be safe to turn on the
lights. They couldn't erase the picture of Morgan with
a rifle.

Suddenly there was a rattling sound from somewhere
nearby. Kate's slender body stiffened in alarm.

"Take Brendan to the attic," she whispered.

"Are you sure?" Bonnie asked.

"Just do it!" came the reply.

Bonnie gathered up the child and ran for the attic
door. She paused at the foot of the stairs to grab the
flashlight and to throw the bolt on the inside of the
door. Afraid to show any light, she crept up the darkened stairs, pulling the frightened and whimpering
child with her. Once in the gloomy attic, she was
tempted to look out the window to see what, in fact,
the police were doing, but she decided to stay away
from the windows.

She crouched with the confused child in a far corner and strained to interpret the sounds drifting up from below. Bonnie knew that Kate wouldn't let Morgan in, but it would be a simple matter to knock out the window beside the door leading to the backyard and effect an entrance.

Surely that was the front door to the center slamming! She could hear Kate's raised voice and a masculine rumble giving answer as she clutched the crying child closer, prepared to use the heavy flashlight as a weapon if need be.

Suddenly there was the sound of knocking on the attic door and she thrust Brendan behind her. But then, over the pounding of her heart, she recognized the voice calling her name. She lifted the chubby child and fairly slid and stumbled down the stairs, where she unbolted the door and threw it open.

In a moment she was in David's arms, with a protesting Brendan squashed between them. Somewhere between laughter and tears, she let Brendan slide to the floor, where he slumped on the bottom step and thrust his thumb into his mouth. She surrendered to David's embrace while he repeated her name and his apologies for frightening her.

"But what are you doing here?" she asked when she could catch her breath.

"My mother called me after she had Ethan safely home. I came right down and spent ten minutes arguing with Andy Boudreau before I could convince him you two shouldn't be alone in here. He's a stubborn man, and he's convinced he can catch Morgan before he even approaches the center, but I just couldn't bear to think of you in here.''

Bonnie realized that she was still circled by David's arms and self-consciously stepped back.

''I'm so glad to see you,'' she said softly.

''Are you sure you're okay?''

''I'm fine. Is there any more news about Brendan's father?''

''That's why I came down. They're saying he went to Donna's mother's house and, when no one answered the door, he shot out all the windows. Fortunately, no one was hurt, but when I heard that, all I could think of was all the glass in this place. Boudreau insists that he'll never get close enough, what with all his men outside, but, then, he doesn't have someone he cares about in here.''

Bonnie's heart warmed at his words, and she was about to slip back into his arms when they both heard voices inside the center. Thinking that Boudreau had come in after him, David lifted Brendan in his arms, and together he and Bonnie followed the sound of conversation into the classroom, where Kate sat on a mat beside a sleeping Freddie. Standing over her was a young man dressed in faded jeans and a camouflage jacket. He turned at the sound of their approach, and Bonnie strained to see his features in the darkened room lighted only by a streetlight outside the building.

"Hey, Dave," the man said as Brendan let out a squeal.

"Daddy!" the child exclaimed as he struggled to free himself from David's grasp.

"Well, Gary, surprised to see you," David said calmly, holding the child tighter.

"You can put my kid down, Dave. I've been waiting a long time to see him."

David took a few wary steps into the room. "Sure, Gary, but there was some talk you might be carrying your rifle with you. I wouldn't want anyone to get hurt."

"Hey, Dave, I don't bring my rifle anywhere around my kid." He held out his empty hands for them to see.

David met Kate's eyes, and she nodded slightly. He set the boy on the floor and watched him run to his father, who dropped to his knees to hug him. Kate rose slowly from the mat and walked across the room to where David stood slightly in front of Bonnie. The man kneeling beside the child took no notice of her movements.

"How did he get in?" David whispered.

"I have no idea. After I let you in, I came back in here to be with Freddie, and I found him standing over the child. Somehow he knew that Brendan was still here."

The three of them watched Gary Morgan rise with Brendan in his arms.

David walked slowly toward Gary. "What are you planning to do, Gary?"

"Well, Dave, I was figuring on just walking out of here with my kid."

"I don't think that's going to work. Have you looked out the window?"

"Yeah, I saw the cop cars, but I've got no quarrel with Boudreau. I'm not armed, and I didn't hurt anybody. I didn't even see Donna."

"Donna's sitting outside in a police car, waiting for Brendan, Gary. She's a little afraid of you because of what happened at her mother's house."

"What happened at her mother's?" Gary looked genuinely surprised.

"We heard that you did some shooting there."

"Never happened, Dave. I haven't been near my mother-in-law's place. Truth is, I've been down in the cellar since before noontime. After I saw my cousin, I called the other day-care centers, and they told me Bren wasn't there, so I knew he was here. I was down the cellar when old Boudreau came down to lock the doors. I just hid myself behind the furnace. He made enough clatter coming down there to wake the dead. I've been hiding there ever since, just waiting for the cops to give up and go home."

"That's not going to happen, Gary. Maybe you just need to talk to Donna—"

"It's almost five o'clock, David," Kate interrupted.

"What does that mean?" Gary asked nervously.

"It means Freddie's dad will be coming to pick him up," David explained. "He's the last child left in the center, and there's a good chance Chief Boudreau will come in with him to talk to Kate."

Gary picked up Brendan and started to back toward the cellar door. David guessed that he had the rifle hidden down there and started to move to intercept him when they all heard a pounding at the front door.

The room was in almost total darkness now, and Bonnie, who was standing unnoticed in a corner, suddenly remembered the flashlight still clutched in her hand. As Kate ran for the door, Bonnie switched on the light and aimed its strong beam straight into Gary's face. Blinded by the light, Gary was frozen in place when the police chief burst into the room. Over his shoulder they could see the frightened face of Freddie's father.

In a matter of moments Gary Morgan was being led off in handcuffs, and Brendan was crying in his young mother's arms.

"Poor Gary," Kate said to David. "He isn't such a bad guy."

"No, he never did shoot up his mother-in-law's house."

"I could have told you that, if you asked me. You should know better than to believe everything you hear in this town, David," the police chief told him.

David grinned in reply and was just turning to Bonnie when an irate voice reached their ears. "What the heck is going on here?'' Laurie Miller brushed past the patrolmen on the steps and flung herself into the room. "I came to pick up Ethan. Where is the darn kid?''

Kate sank down wearily onto the mat. "David, I think you should handle this.''

For the first time Bonnie saw David's mouth tighten in anger. The last they saw of Laurie, she was being hustled through the door by a furious David.

"I don't think Laurie will be picking up Ethan anymore,'' Kate commented casually. She pulled herself to her feet. "I'm going to call Mark. He must have heard a million rumors by now and be worried sick. The chief made me unplug the phones after I reached all the parents.''

Kate was still in her office, reassuring her husband, when David came back into the center. Bonnie was hesitant to mention Laurie, so instead she asked, "Are the police gone?''

"Yes. I hope they won't be too hard on Gary. I really feel sorry for the guy.''

"Me too,'' Bonnie said. She poked her head into Kate's office, where Kate was hanging up the phone and locking her desk. "Do you need me for anything?'' she asked.

"No, go on along home. That's where I'm going, and I'm going to soak in a hot tub until I turn into a prune.''

"Sounds wonderful,'' Bonnie said, slipping into her denim jacket.

Bonnie and David walked hand in hand to the door and down the center steps. When they reached Bonnie's car, David asked, "Can I sit with you for a minute?"

"Of course," she answered. They sat for a moment in silence.

"I don't know how to thank you for coming to the center tonight," Bonnie began.

"I couldn't stay away." He took her hand and gently stroked her fingers. "I've missed you the last few weeks. I wish things were different, but as long as Caroline is making this effort with Ethan. . . ."

Bonnie stiffened. "What you're telling me is that nothing has changed."

"I'm afraid not," he said miserably.

"Well, in that case, I'd really like to get home. I'm very tired, and I'm sure you'll excuse me." Bonnie ignored the expression on David's face as he left the car.

When Bonnie arrived at the farm, she found Liz and Tim anxiously waiting for her. They each hugged her warmly and then ushered her into the kitchen, where Liz had a huge pot of stew bubbling on the stove.

"Are you all right? Are you sure you're all right?" Liz asked. "You're the talk of the town, you know. We've been calling the police station every half hour, but we couldn't get any information. Tim even went down to the center and tried to talk that dumb ox into letting him in, but no dice."

Tim grinned. "What a way to talk about our illustrious paragon of law and order!"

"That's nothing compared to what Tim called him when he talked to poor Mark Hollander, especially when they found out that Gary had been in there since noontime!"

"How did you find out so quickly?" Bonnie asked.

"Tim was outside the whole time. He kept calling Mark and me from the phone booth at the gas station. He wasn't going to leave there until you were out safe. He didn't come home until he saw them taking Gary away in cuffs."

Bonnie looked at Tim in surprise. She was so touched that for the first time in that long, frightening day, her eyes filled with tears. Tim ducked his head in embarrassment.

"Liz, how about dishing up some of that stew? Bonnie looks like she could use a good meal."

Liz obligingly ladled fragrant servings of stew into bowls. "Okay," she said, "she can eat, but then she's going to tell us exactly what happened, word for word." She plunked herself down opposite Bonnie expectantly.

Chapter Eleven

After dinner Bonnie called Faith to tell her firsthand what had happened at the center. By the time she had related all the details for the second time, she was so exhausted that she followed Kate's advice and soaked in a hot tub until the tension flowed from her body and her fingers and toes wrinkled like prunes.

In the morning the center still buzzed with excitement. Brendan was not there, and Kate informed the staff that his mom had taken him to visit friends for a few days. Because of the extreme sensitivity of their students, Bonnie and Faith had to make a concerted effort to restore a normal schedule and a calm environment.

Despite their joint efforts Ethan had a terrible day. Bonnie couldn't help but wonder if Laurie had in fact managed to take him from his grandmother's house and deliver him to Caroline. Had Ethan spent the evening with his mother? Perhaps Kate could find out.

By noontime Ethan had reduced both of the little girls to tears by destroying their artwork and had terrorized poor Joel by snatching toys from his hands. Lunch was reduced to a shambles when Ethan decided to walk across the table and kick over the juice. In desperation Bonnie pulled the protesting child to Kate's office, while Faith dealt with the soggy sandwiches.

"We need help," Bonnie announced, sinking into the orange chair with the struggling child on her lap.

"I see that," Kate said mildly. She rose from her chair and approached Ethan. She bent over him and took his small face between her palms and directed his gaze to her face.

"Ethan," she said softly, "you need to calm down. Look at me, Ethan. You need to be a nice, quiet boy."

"Has he had lunch?" she asked.

Bonnie told her what had happened to lunch.

"Okay, leave him with me. It's almost his naptime. I'll try to get him settled, and then we can talk."

Reluctantly Bonnie returned to the other children. She found that Faith had rescued lunch and restored the others to good spirits. "I feel terrible," Bonnie confided to her.

"Don't," Faith reassured her. "Kate doesn't mind. Something is happening with Ethan that we don't understand. It's her job to find out what."

"But we should be able to handle him."

"We have the other children to consider. He's not our only student."

Bonnie had to agree, but it hurt her to relinquish Ethan to anyone else's care, even Kate's. She watched while Kate sat on the edge of Ethan's mat and rubbed his back until he fell into an uneasy sleep. She expected Kate to call her into the office for a conference, but, to her surprise, Kate slipped into her jacket and left the center.

Bonnie found Martha lulling her babies to sleep. "Did Kate have a meeting today?" she asked her.

"Not that I know of," she answered. "Has she left the building?"

"Yes, she just zipped off without a word."

Martha shrugged. "Well, not to worry. I'm sure she won't be long."

But Kate was gone most of the afternoon, and when she returned, she looked pale and angry. She returned to find Bonnie and Faith struggling with Ethan, who had removed most of his clothes. "Let me help you get him dressed," she offered. "David is picking him up in a few minutes."

"Did you go to see him?" Faith asked, stuffing Ethan's leg into his overalls.

"I've been everywhere. I spent some time with Helen Anderson, dropped in on Caroline, where I was subjected to Laurie Miller, and spent the last hour with David."

"And what did you learn?" Bonnie asked.

''A few things, but not enough. For one thing, Ethan was with his mother last night. Laurie did go from here to Helen's, where she convinced her that she had David's permission to take him to his mother.''

By now they had the child fully dressed again, and Bonnie sat down to take him into her lap. He had slipped into a lethargic state and was content to twirl a lock of her hair through his fingers. Bonnie pressed a kiss on his cheek, and he didn't pull away.

''Why does Laurie always pick up Ethan? Why doesn't Caroline come for him herself?'' Bonnie asked curiously.

Kate flashed her dimpled smile. ''That's one of the things I asked, but Caroline only hedged, and I didn't get an answer.''

''Did you get any impression of what might be going on at Laurie's house?''

''It's hard to tell. Laurie has two children of her own, regular little hellions, but I got the feeling they weren't very interested in Ethan.''

Bonnie sighed in frustration and cuddled Ethan, who seemed to have fallen into a doze.

''I asked David to come for Ethan and spend some time with him alone. I don't know if it will help, but the child is obviously overstimulated and needs some quiet time,'' Kate told her.

''I think you're right, but if it doesn't work, will we be able to keep him here at the center?''

"That's the problem. I must say, Helen is frantic. She's afraid he will have to be institutionalized."

"Surely that's not a possibility?"

"Not at the moment, but we have to consider the other children. A few more days like today. . . ."

Bonnie was about to protest when she heard David approaching. He stood for a moment, looking down at her with Ethan cuddled in her arms, and then turned his worried gaze to Kate. "Is he all right?" he asked.

"For the moment," Kate said briskly. "I haven't had a chance to tell Bonnie about the meeting."

Bonnie's heart sank. *Another meeting*, she thought. "What did you have in mind?"

"As I told David, I'd like Caroline to come to the center while Ethan is here and watch him interact with some of the children."

Bonnie tried to hide her surprise. Ethan didn't interact with the children, as Kate knew very well. Even David looked dubious but was too worried to argue. "Caroline will be here tomorrow about two o'clock," she continued. "I'd like you to be here, too, David."

David nodded his head in agreement and squatted down to take Ethan from Bonnie's arms. He smiled shyly at her, as if uncertain of her reaction. "Then I'll see you tomorrow," he said softly.

When David had gone, Bonnie turned to Kate. "Pardon me, but what was that all about? Since when does Ethan interact with the other children?"

"Sorry, Bonnie, I'm surprised you were able to keep

a straight face. Actually, the only interaction I hope to see will be between Ethan and his mother, if such a thing exists. Maybe we'll learn something.'' She shrugged. ''We've nothing to lose, right?''

Bonnie had to agree, but as the time for the meeting approached on the next afternoon, she became more and more apprehensive. Fortunately, Ethan was calmer that day. Bonnie and Faith planned some activities for the children that would include involvement by Caroline, and the little girls were excited by the prospect of a visitor.

When Caroline arrived, she was dressed more casually than on her previous visit, but she was still exquisite in her pressed jeans and brightly patterned sweater. Her shining blond hair was pulled into a ponytail, and her pale face was lightly made up. She smiled with great charm at Tina and Pammy but was hesitant in the face of Freddie's exuberant handshake.

Since the girls were so clearly delighted to have Caroline in their midst, Bonnie allowed them to pick the first activity for the afternoon, and they chose the dress-up box. They led a smiling Caroline to a large wooden chest that held an assortment of castoffs and odd garments that the children loved to don and play make-believe.

She was quick to help Tina into a trailing skirt and sequined blouse while Pammy chose a lace-trimmed prom gown of some long-past era. Joel struggled into a fringed vest, so Faith placed a cowboy hat on his head, and Bonnie tied a red bandanna around Freddie's chubby neck and thrust an engineer's cap over his dark bangs. While the girls paraded around grandly, the boys giggled and pointed fingers at each other and then switched hats.

In the meantime Ethan stood stolidly at the edge of the group, anxiously twisting his fingers together. Bonnie said quietly to Caroline, "Ethan will sometimes wear the magician's cloak. Why don't you put it on him?"

Caroline turned from adjusting Pammy's skirt. "Oh, Bonnie, perhaps you should help him. He's used to you."

Bonnie shrugged and placed the cape around Ethan's shoulders. He accepted it stoically and moved a little closer to his mother and the laughing children. Bonnie excused herself when she noticed that David had arrived and was talking quietly with Kate.

She greeted him casually and then asked Kate, "Is there anything special you would like us to do with Ethan today?"

"No, just continue with your usual activities as long as you're able to include Caroline. David and I will just observe, if that's all right with you."

"That's fine, but are you sure you wouldn't care to join us for finger painting?" she asked David.

"I think I'll pass," he said with his quick grin.

Feeling slightly flustered, Bonnie returned to the children to find Caroline applying rouge to the girls' cheeks while the boys played cowboy with Faith. Ethan stood enveloped in the black cloak, oblivious to the activity around him.

"Let's put the clothes away now," Bonnie announced. "We'll show Ethan's mommy how well we finger paint."

Faith was already setting out the paper and paints when the children had finished folding the clothes and had returned them to the trunk. Bonnie helped the boys put on the oversized shirts they used to cover their clothes and was handing Ethan's shirt to Caroline when Pammy said she needed to go to the bathroom.

Faith was about to take her, but Caroline spoke up. "Oh, I'll take her. I'd like to." She thrust Ethan's shirt back at Bonnie and walked off with the little girl.

Bonnie scowled as she pushed Ethan's arms into the cover-up. She met Faith's eyes and watched her purse her lips.

When Caroline brought Pammy back, Bonnie offered her a plastic cape to put over her clothes, knowing how messy the paints could be, and she accepted with a laugh, seating herself between the girls. The children attacked the paper with their usual abandon, and soon everyone was in paint to their elbows, including Ethan, who chose to work exclusively in red. When it was time to clean up, neither Bonnie nor Faith was surprised when Caroline chose to escort Pammy and Tina to the bathroom, leaving the boys in their care.

"So much for interaction," Bonnie muttered. "Are you getting a picture here?"

"Ethan's mother never touches him," Faith replied.

When the well-scrubbed girls returned, it was time for three of the children to go home. Kate and David joined the group as Caroline was hugging Pammy and Tina good-bye and waving to Joel. Bonnie noticed an odd expression on Kate's face. She was holding Ethan's jacket, and after she had exchanged a few words with Tina's mother, she turned to Caroline.

"Ethan's done so well today, we thought you might like to take him along home." She extended the jacket to Caroline, who looked at it helplessly. She looked appealingly at David.

"Why don't you put his jacket on while I get my bag?"

As she turned to go, Ethan brushed past her to reach his father, and she recoiled slightly. Kate's eyes narrowed, and Bonnie held her breath, but when Kate spoke, it was softly.

"Caroline, you're afraid of Ethan, aren't you? You're physically afraid of him."

A flush started on Caroline's neck and moved over her alabaster skin in unbecoming blotches. "Yes, I am," she said defiantly.

Faith scooped Ethan from the floor and carried him to the next room, where she dumped the blocks on the floor in front of him and Freddie.

Bonnie wondered if she should leave, too, but Kate placed a restraining hand on her arm.

"I wasn't always frightened by him. At first I really tried to take care of him, but every time I touched him, he would start that stupid spinning, or he'd make those weird noises."

Bonnie watched a muscle twitch in David's jaw, but he didn't speak.

"Is that why you never picked him up from the center?" Kate asked.

"Of course! I couldn't even strap him into his car seat! Laurie offered to do it. She can handle him. Even at the house she took over. She doesn't take any nonsense." Caroline babbled on, unable to stop once started.

"Why didn't you tell me?" David asked.

She turned as if she had forgotten he was there. Her face visibly softened as she looked up at him, and her pale-blue eyes filled with sudden tears. "Oh, David, I didn't want you to know." She put her hand on his arm.

"I think you two need to talk," Kate said dryly. "Why don't you leave Ethan here and come back for him at the usual time, David?"

"I think you're right," he answered, walking away from Caroline without a glance at either her or Bonnie.

Caroline grabbed her coat and ran after him, catching him at the door. Bonnie watched them leave together, unable to hear what Caroline was saying so earnestly.

For a moment she felt rooted to the spot; then Kate spoke briskly. "Come into my office for a minute."

Bonnie followed Kate into the cramped office and took her place in the orange chair. She noticed her hands trembling and clutched them in her lap.

"Well, we have an answer of sorts, don't we?" Kate asked.

"Did you see this coming? I must admit I didn't have a clue until today."

"When I spoke to her at Laurie Miller's house, I noticed that she left most of his care to her sister, but I hoped it was just because I was there and she didn't want to interrupt our conversation. Watching her here, though, it became very clear."

"It seems like more than fear, doesn't it?"

"You're right; it's more like an aversion. She really can't bear to be near him."

"This will break David's heart," Bonnie remarked.

"Nonsense. David's tougher than that. He was doing fine as a single parent, and he can do it again. It will be a relief to know what was troubling Ethan, poor rejected child. Now all David has to do is get the guts to deal with Caroline for the second time."

"And will he be able to do that?"

"Well, that's the question, isn't it?" Kate replied, and the two women sat in silence until Faith knocked at the door.

"Is someone going to tell me what happened?" she asked plaintively.

"Sorry, Faith, I'm coming," Bonnie said.

It seemed like hours until David returned to take Ethan home. When he did come, he was pale and distracted. When Bonnie handed him Ethan's journal, he mumbled his thanks and turned to leave without a word.

Bonnie reached out to detain him. "David," she said softly, "Is there anything I can do to help?"

He seemed surprised by her words. She took a deep breath and continued, "I've missed you, David. I've missed our time together."

"I've missed you, too, Bonnie, you know I have. And you're right—I need to talk to someone about Ethan and his mother. But it's not fair to involve you in all this. I thought perhaps Kate. . . ."

Bonnie stiffened, but something made her persist. "If you want to talk about Ethan, I'm his teacher. I'm sure I can help you."

"I'm sure you can, but try to understand, I can't be with you."

"You can't?"

"Not until I straighten things out with Caroline. It wouldn't be fair to you."

"But I don't mind. I want to be with you."

"Bonnie, you just don't get it. It's not that I don't want to be with you. It's that I can't." And, with that, he took the journal from her hand and went to find Ethan.

* * *

That weekend Bonnie went home to visit her parents. She had told her mother briefly about David without going into too much detail, and her mother had been tactful enough not to press her. Now she was able to relate to her parents the story of Gary Morgan's invasion of the center, being careful to make light of the danger she and Kate might have been in.

When she had finished, her father excused himself and went down to the basement, where he was refinishing an old dresser. After he was safely gone, her mother said, "And your David came to be with you?"

"He's not my David, but, yes, he did come, and we were very happy to see him."

"I should think so! You know, Bonnie, he sounds like a very good man."

"He is, Mom."

"And I think he cares for you very much, no matter what he says."

"Do you really think so?"

"Well, Bonnie, I wouldn't say this in front of your father, since he really doesn't approve of your seeing a divorced man, but this David sounds like a very caring person, someone worth fighting for."

"Mom! I'm surprised to hear you say that," Bonnie said with a grin.

"I'm surprised myself. Shh! Here comes Dad." They could hear Patrick Delaney's footsteps on the cellar stairs. He paused in the doorway. ''Put another coat on that old dresser, Bonnie. Maybe you can use it someday when you get an apartment.'' He looked from one flushed face to another. ''Well, I won't interrupt your girl talk, but, Bonnie, I must say, that David of yours sounds like a very good man. Now, what are you two giggling about?''

Bonnie left for New Hampshire late Sunday afternoon. She wanted to be back in time for supper with Liz and Tim. Liz was still offering supper to her guests but had promised to stop after hunting season was over. Bonnie knew she could use her help. Besides, Liz and Tim felt like family now. When Bonnie hugged her mother good-bye, she promised to come home for Thanksgiving. She knew it would mean a lot to her parents, although Liz had already invited her to spend the holiday at the farm.

The weather was turning colder, so Bonnie packed her down parka and her heavy sweaters. She also put her typewriter in the backseat of the car along with some college catalogs. It was time to think about enrolling in some courses toward her master's degree.

Liz was most grateful for her help, and after the hunters were safely on their way and Joshua was tucked up in his crib, the two women settled down in the den. Tim had excused himself and headed off to bed since he had to be up at the crack of dawn for a trip to the market to purchase fresh produce.

''How are your folks?'' Liz asked.

"Good. I think my father is really looking forward to retiring; he has so many projects lined up."

"Will your mom mind having him underfoot?"

"I don't think so. They have a wonderful marriage. I hope I do as well. But, speaking of my mother, you won't believe what she told me." Bonnie related her mother's advice about fighting for David, but Liz was not the least surprised.

"Your mother's a smart lady, and she's got the right idea."

"Oh, really, and what do you suggest I do about David?"

"Come right out and tell him how you feel. What have you got to lose?"

"My self-respect?" Bonnie inquired.

"An overrated commodity, in my book," Liz answered.

Chapter Twelve

Bonnie gave a lot of thought to Liz's advice, but she wondered if she would ever have the chance to use it. When she arrived at the center on Monday morning, she found that David had come and gone. Kate handed her Ethan's journal without a word. She quickly scanned David's account of the weekend to find that he had kept Ethan quietly at home. It was obvious from Ethan's calm and controlled behavior that this was exactly what he needed. The blue shadows were gone from his cheeks, his nervous tics were at a minimum, and while he did not exactly play with the other children, he copied their activities with little fuss.

At lunchtime Kate called Bonnie into her office. "I thought you would like to know, Brendan will be back tomorrow."

"I'm glad to hear that. I've missed him. What will happen to his father, do you know?"

"Well, David went to his hearing to speak up for him. The judge was very understanding. Gary's on probation, and Donna has agreed to allow him visitation rights with Brendan, under supervision."

"That was good of David. Were they friends?"

"They went to high school together, but more than that, I think David could relate to him as a father."

"I hope it works out for the Morgans," Bonnie said.

"I think it will, but what about you?"

"Me?" Bonnie asked.

"You don't look very happy today. I hope it's not the job, because I was about to tell you how pleased I am with your work."

Bonnie blushed slightly. "Thank you, that's good to hear. I did have some doubts about my effectiveness with Ethan, but I love the job and really enjoy the children."

"Good, because I would hate to lose you. In fact, I may be depending on you more than ever." Kate paused, causing Bonnie to raise an eyebrow in question.

"I hope you can keep a secret," Kate continued. Bonnie nodded in affirmation. "It's a little early for a general announcement, but it looks like I'm pregnant."

Bonnie smiled in delight. "That's wonderful! I'm so happy for you."

"Thanks, but the truth is, I'm not feeling awfully

well, and I don't know what to expect this time, so I hope you'll be able to fill in for me sometimes.''

"I'd be glad to help any way I can."

"That's a relief. Oh, and, Bonnie, I will tell Faith my news before the day is over. I can't expect you to work with her all day and keep such an interesting secret."

"Thank you. It would be impossible to keep it from her. Sometimes I think she reads minds."

"You're right. I wouldn't be surprised to find she already knows," Kate agreed. "But that doesn't answer my question. Since it's not the job that's worrying you, it must be a personal matter and none of my business."

"It's personal, but hardly a secret. I'm concerned about my relationship with David. People are telling me to fight for him, but I don't know how."

"When you say 'people,' I'm sure you include Liz. That sounds like her style."

"Yes, but she's not the only one."

"Well, I'm not big on giving advice, but I do know David fairly well, and I would suggest you be honest with him."

"That seems to be the consensus."

"I do sympathize. I must admit I was quite timid about sharing my feelings with Mark, and if the truth be told, Liz almost lost Tim because he was afraid that a city girl would not be happy in such a small town."

"She never mentioned that."

"Ask her about it. I don't mean to minimize your problem, but women often have to nudge men along."

"Just don't ask me what I have to lose," Bonnie said with a smile.

"Oh, no, I understand perfectly, but you need to ask yourself, is it worth it?"

"When you put it that way, of course, the answer is yes."

"Well, then, good luck," Kate said as Bonnie rose from the orange chair.

Even with her new resolution, Bonnie wondered when she would have the chance to tell David how she felt about him. He was clearly avoiding her, and as the cool, dark days of November passed, she could only wonder what was happening between David and Caroline.

Bonnie knew that Caroline was still in town, although neither she nor Laurie Miller had permission to take Ethan from the center. Occasionally Helen Anderson picked up the boy, but if she knew what was happening, she didn't share that information with Bonnie.

Finally, the Monday before Thanksgiving, Laurie Miller surprised them all by appearing at the center. Bonnie and Faith were just settling the children at the picnic table for lunch.

"Well, I hope you're satisfied, you little—"

"Excuse me," Kate interrupted, hurrying from her

office. "I don't think you have any business here with my teachers."

"I wasn't talking to you," Laurie announced haughtily. "I'm talking to her." She jerked a finger in Bonnie's direction. "Thanks to her, my sister is leaving town again. She would have gotten David back again if it weren't for her."

Bonnie's heart sang at this information, but she hid her elation and answered calmly, "I hardly think the trouble Caroline had with Ethan had anything to do with me."

"Oh, really." Laurie's tone dripped with sarcasm. "I don't suppose your making time with her husband had anything to do with it, either."

"I think that's enough of that," Kate said firmly, grasping Laurie by the arm. "I'm going to have to ask you to leave."

"I'm going, all right, but I just want her to know, she's not getting much of a bargain. That David is such a wimp, he'll never make up his mind. Caroline's better off without him!" With that, she hurried out the door.

Bonnie and Faith looked stunned, but Kate just laughed. "I haven't seen an exit like that since the witch in *The Wizard of Oz*. I almost went in search of a bucket of water!"

"Do you suppose she was telling the truth about Caroline?" Faith asked.

"Probably so. I almost feel sorry for Laurie. She must be lonely since her folks moved to Florida. She really wanted her sister to stay in town,'' Kate answered.

"If only Caroline could have loved Ethan as we do! I'm sure David would have given her visitation rights,'' Faith commented.

"I don't think that's all Caroline wanted,'' Kate said.

"You're probably right, but now she's lost it all,'' Faith answered.

"Don't waste your sympathy, my kindhearted friend,'' Kate said, hugging Faith warmly. "Caroline always lands on her feet. I'm sure she's already working on a new plan.''

Faith looked at Bonnie, who hadn't said a word. "As long as it doesn't include David,'' she added wisely.

Bonnie found it difficult to concentrate on her work for the rest of that day. When David came to pick up Ethan, she looked at him inquiringly, but his face was unreadable. They exchanged a few words about Ethan's behavior, which was slowly improving, but nothing of a personal nature. Bonnie watched him walk away with feelings of frustration and anger.

That night at dinner, Liz was gleeful. She had already heard the news that Caroline was leaving town and couldn't resist the temptation to urge Bonnie to action. Even Tim's constant admonitions to mind her own business had no effect on her. She was so ebullient that Bonnie could only laugh and join in her mad schemes, which ranged from sending David singing telegrams to bombing his house with water balloons.

"Wouldn't a simple phone call do?" Tim asked dryly, trying to restore a measure of sanity to the conversation.

"Too unimaginative," Liz chided.

"Tim, if you were David, how would you like me to approach you?"

"Well, I'm not sure, but I think what happened was that the more time that passed since you two were together, the more awkward David began to feel. Now he probably isn't sure if you still care about him or have just given up."

Liz brightened visibly. "In that case, maybe a nice man-to-man phone call from you would do the trick!"

"No way! I'm not going to interfere in Bonnie's life no matter how you justify it."

"But Tim," Bonnie said with her most winning smile, "it wouldn't be interfering if I knew you were doing it."

"Nice try, Bonnie. Liz must be giving you lessons." He rose to take his cup and dessert plate to the sink.

"That was good, Bonnie. For a moment there I thought it was going to work."

"Me too," Bonnie said with a sigh.

"Don't worry, you'll think of something," Liz replied.

And that night, when she couldn't sleep, Bonnie formulated a plan, a bold plan, that she didn't even share with Liz. All the next day at work, she hugged her secret to herself, and if Faith noticed that she often smiled for no reason, she didn't comment.

When her workday finally ended, she popped into the office to say good-night to Kate.

"How are you feeling?" Bonnie asked quietly.

"Very tired, but otherwise okay," Kate answered. "By the way, Bonnie, have you decided to go home for Thanksgiving?"

"Yes, I promised my mom I would be there. The whole family will be together this year, and my folks are really looking forward to it."

"Sounds wonderful," Kate said, suppressing a yawn. "Excuse me, I can't seem to stay awake. I wish I could let you go early tomorrow, but I gave the volunteers the day off, so we'll be short-staffed."

"That's all right, I don't mind staying until my regular time."

"All right then. I'll see you in the morning. By the way, you're looking very cheerful today. Big plans for tonight?"

"You might say that," Bonnie replied with an airy wave.

By the time she emerged from the office, David had hustled Ethan off, after getting his journal from Jennifer.

"You just missed David again," Jennifer told her in an exasperated tone.

"That's all right," Bonnie assured her.

"No it's not," Jennifer said, obviously frustrated by the lack of progress in a romance for which she had such high hopes.

Bonnie just smiled at the girl, secure in the knowledge of her plan. She left the center and drove to the neighboring city of Milford, where she did some shopping. She placed her purchases carefully in the backseat of the Nova and drove back to Abbots Hill.

A half mile past the center, she turned onto a country road that wound its way uphill, past a dairy farm and a private school.

Finally she turned onto Prescott Lane and stopped in front of a small Cape Cod house. The road was dark without streetlights, but a gas lantern glowed on the front lawn, and the path, paved with white pebbles, was clearly defined. She could see the red truck parked in the driveway as she opened the back door of the car and carefully removed her purchases. Slowly she walked up the path to David's house.

Bonnie stood for a moment on the top step and remembered the one time she had been in this house. It was the day David chose to show her Temple Mountain. He had picked her up at the farm and then discovered that he had forgotten his camera, so they stopped back at his house to pick it up. Because Ethan was spending the afternoon with his grandparents, Bonnie had hesitated a moment when David invited her into the house. But she had accompanied him, and while he ran upstairs, she couldn't resist the temptation to look around his home.

The living room was simply furnished in warm colors and durable fabrics. What she could see of the kitchen from where she stood at the front door was tidy and functional. The pile of toys and blocks in the corner gave testimony to the small boy who lived there.

When David rattled down the stairs, he had smiled to find her rooted to the doormat. "You could have looked around," he said, his eyes crinkling at the corners. "Would you like to see the house?" he asked.

"I'd love to." She followed him into the kitchen with its maple table and chairs and its wide window opening onto a wooded yard. A pine tree close to the house was festooned with birdhouses and feeders accommodating a variety of chickadees and finches.

"Ethan likes to watch the birds," David had said then with a touch of sadness in his voice. "Come, let me show you his room."

Bonnie preceded David up the stairs. The door at the head of the stairs was closed. "My room," David commented, walking down the hall. At the back of the house, overlooking the yard, was a square room painted a pale blue. When Bonnie looked up, she saw that the ceiling had been painted a deeper blue and that white clouds had been stenciled over the bed. The walls were covered with bright prints, and the floor was covered with a hooked rug. The tracks of a small train were set up along its outer edge.

"It's charming," she had said, wondering if she was seeing the results of Caroline's loving care.

"Thank you. I did it over last year when I moved him out of his crib." David answered her unspoken question. Back in the hall, he gestured toward another closed door. "Combination storage and guest room," he explained, "not that we get much company." He led her back down the stairs, where they stood awkwardly in the living room for a moment.

"We'd better go," David finally said, taking her hand.

Reluctantly Bonnie had left the warm little house, but now she stood on the steps, frightened but tingling with excitement.

She had gotten her wonderful idea from an old movie she would watch every year with her mother. The movie was called *Easter Parade*, and in it Judy Garland, in an effort to woo Fred Astaire, had sent him candy, flowers, and a top hat with a live rabbit inside. Considering the upcoming holiday, Bonnie had settled on a foot-high chocolate turkey and a bouquet of flowers with balloons attached. Now she clutched these in her hands and firmly rang the bell.

When David opened the door, his face was a study in consternation and dismay. "Bonnie? I can't believe it's you."

Bonnie smiled broadly, oblivious to his distress. "Can I come in?" she asked gaily.

Just then a familiar voice wafted down the stairs behind him.

"David, did I hear the bell? Tell her to go away; we're busy here."

The smile froze on Bonnie's face. There was no mistaking Caroline's breathy tones. She thrust the flowers and the turkey into David's hands, and while he fumbled to get a hold on the candy turkey, she turned and ran for her car.

Humiliated and heartbroken, she hardly heard him call her name.

"Bonnie, please wait. It's not what you think."

All she could hear was her own heart pounding in her ears and the sound of her own sobs.

Bonnie couldn't bear to return to the farm and face Liz and Tim. She stopped at a phone booth and called Liz to tell her that she had some shopping to do and wouldn't be home for dinner. She didn't give Liz a chance to ask questions.

Then Bonnie drove back to Milford and found a diner frequented by truckers and construction workers. Assuming that she wouldn't meet anyone she knew, she lingered over a man-sized hamburger and coffee until the friendly waitress grew curious and began to hover in her vicinity.

When she could toy with her food no longer, she left a generous tip, paid for the food she had barely touched, and left. It was still only seven o'clock, so she drove to the nearest movie theater and chose a show at random.

Somewhere she had heard that *Dances With Wolves* was a very long movie. Despite herself she fell under the spell of the glorious music and scenery and for a few hours was suspended in time, free from the grief and embarrassment her ill-conceived plan had brought upon her. But eventually the movie was over, and she had to return to reality.

When she reached the farm, she could hear the sounds of the television from the den, so she called out a greeting to Liz and Tim. Liz invited her to join them, but she begged off, saying she was too tired and was going straight to bed.

After a tearful and sleepless night, Bonnie arrived at the breakfast table, pale and heavy-eyed.

"Are you okay?" Liz asked.

"I'm fine," she lied.

Liz regarded her with obvious disbelief but for once held her tongue.

"I'll be going to my folks' house this evening, but I'll see you before I go," Bonnie continued, putting her dishes in the dishwasher.

"That's fine. Why don't you stop at the store and take some pumpkins for the kids?"

"Thanks, Liz. I'll see you then." Bonnie slipped into her jacket and listlessly walked to her car.

As she approached the center, she realized that she

would probably see David, but she was so demoralized by what she perceived to be a mortifying experience that she wasn't sure she cared.

When she did, in fact, meet David on the worn steps to the center, she could only turn her eyes away from his gaze. But David simply murmured her name while pressing Ethan's journal into her nerveless fingers. Before she could speak, he was gone.

Once inside the center, she couldn't resist opening the journal. To her surprise, a sheet of blue stationery fluttered to the floor. Printed on it, in David's neat hand, was the following poem:

She walks in beauty, like the night
Of cloudless climes and starry skies,
And all that's best of dark and bright
Meet in her aspect and her eyes;
Thus mellow'd to that tender light
Which heaven to gaudy day denies.

Lord Byron

Bonnie read the poem several times. A mix of emotions washed over her. Touched by the beauty of the poem, she felt a glow of optimism, quickly followed by anger and disappointment. Was David playing games with her? Obviously his relationship with Caroline wasn't over, as evidenced by her presence on the second floor of his house. Maybe Laurie Miller was right. Maybe David would never make up his mind.

She stuffed the note into her pocket and tried to put it out of her mind.

Of course, she was unsuccessful. While she worked with her children on this the last day before the holiday, while she colored turkeys and fashioned Indian head-dresses, while she served applesauce and carrot sticks, David's voice spoke in her ear; his blue eyes smiled into hers.

When, to her surprise, Ethan consented to sit on her lap for a few moments, she couldn't resist kissing his smooth blond head. For a moment she was almost frightened. She loved this child so much, but if she couldn't resolve the situation with his father, how could she continue to work at the center? And what of her commitment to Kate?

But through the whole dreadful day, she had to keep up the pretense of normalcy for the children and for Kate, who had problems of her own.

By five o'clock she was exhausted. She had already packed her car for the trip to Massachusetts, and she had only to stop at the store to pick up the pumpkins. She said her good-byes to the staff at the center and convinced Faith that she should deliver Ethan and his journal to David. Faith gave her a puzzled look but complied.

Finally Bonnie was ready to leave. Even though she was tired, she was looking forward to the long drive, when she could be totally alone and able to let her guard down. When she left the center, the small parking lot was deep in shadows. For a moment she was frightened to see a tall figure leaning against her car. She froze a few feet from the Nova and was about to return to the center when she recognized the red truck in the driveway and the small boy in the passenger seat. Slowly she approached the man waiting for her.

"Bonnie," he said simply.

"Hi, David," she answered.

"Did you get the poem?"

"Yes, I did, but I'm not sure what it meant."

"Quite simply, it meant that I've been a fool and I want a chance to make it up to you." He took her hand and held it between his warm palms.

"I don't understand. Yesterday, when I came to your house. . . ." Just the memory made her blush with embarrassment.

"That's what I came to explain. Caroline was at the house to pick up some things she had stored there. When you came to the door, she thought it was her sister, Laurie, and she was just being funny. I tried to explain, but you took off like a frightened deer."

"You mean she wasn't there with you?"

"Of course not. It's been over between Caroline and me for a very long time. I told you that."

"I know you did, but when she came back to town, I thought . . . she's so beautiful."

"Is she? I don't see it anymore. I have eyes for someone else." His hand traveled up her arm. "Forgive me for taking so long, but I was so worried about

Ethan, and with Caroline and her sister aggravating me. . . . Well, it's no excuse, but I was waiting for everything to be perfect." He bent his head to look into her face. "Do you forgive me for being such a dope?"

Bonnie nodded just before David took her in his arms and kissed her gently. After a few moments he whispered against her cheek, "Stay with us for Thanksgiving. Stay with Ethan and me."

Bonnie pulled back and looked into his eyes. With regret she answered, "I can't. I promised my mom I would be with the family."

He pulled her back into his arms. "I understand, but come back soon."

"I'll be back on Friday, I promise," she answered, returning his embrace with enthusiasm.

"Good. We'll be waiting for you. My mother will be disappointed. She had hoped you could spend Thanksgiving with the family. She's very anxious to get to know the woman I intend to marry."

Bonnie pulled back in surprise but was reassured by the warmth of David's gaze. She had no need to answer him with words. Her expression told him everything he wished to know. Over his shoulder she saw Ethan turn his head, and maybe it was an illusion of shadows on the glass, but for a moment she was sure she saw Ethan smile.